THE VAMPIRE PLAGUES

BOOK THREE
MEXICO, 1850

THE VAMPIRE PLAGUES

BOOK THREE
MEXICO, 1850

BY SEBASTIAN ROOK

With special thanks to Ben Jeapes

SCHOLASTIC INC.

New York   Toronto   London   Auckland   Sydney
Mexico City   New Delhi   Hong Kong   Buenos Aires

ISBN 0-439-63394-X
Text copyright © 2005 by Working Partners Ltd.

Design by Steve Scott

12 11 10 9 8 7 6 5 4 3 2   5 6 7 8 9 10/0
Printed in the U.S.A.   40
First printing, October 2005

THE VAMPIRE PLAGUES

BOOK THREE
MEXICO, 1850

CHAPTER ONE

The Gulf of Mexico stretched as far as the eye could see in every direction. The schooner *Providence* sped across the sea, her sails curved and taut in the wind. The ship's bow sliced cleanly through the waves with bursts of white spray. Perched at the top of the mainmast, Jack Harkett whooped with glee.

Jack had asked one of the sailors to show him how to climb the rigging almost as soon as the *Providence* had left New Orleans. He loved it up here. The fresh breeze ruffled his dark brown hair. His face and neck were tanned. He was barefoot, wearing a linen shirt and canvas trousers, and he had never felt more alive or free.

He hadn't realized the Gulf was so big, but he had soon learned that it was more than a thousand miles across at its widest point. They were already well into the second day of their journey and there was no land in sight. New Orleans was far behind them to the north, and the Yucatán peninsula—their destination in Mexico—lay ahead.

The Yucatán. Once, the name had meant nothing to Jack. Now it meant danger and death and vampires. He knew the region was thick with dense jungle and scattered with ruins left by the ancient Mayan people. And he knew that a dark force had once ruled there—a god who demanded the blood of human sacrifice. A god whose bloodlust had weakened the once-powerful civilization and ultimately destroyed the empire. The Mayans had vanished, their cities had crumbled, and the god, Camazotz, had fallen into forgotten legend. His name meant little to anyone nowadays, save in shadowy corners of Mexico where it was still whispered with fear.

Jack had come face-to-face with Camazotz and his vampire servants. Not in the depths of the Yucatán jungle but in London, and then again in Paris. Camazotz's plague of vampires had threatened both cities until the ancient god had been defeated by Jack and his friends Ben and Emily Cole.

In Paris they had learned that Camazotz was intent on finding and assembling the four pieces of an amulet that would give him power beyond imagining. He had already obtained three of those pieces. The friends had left France one step ahead of their enemy, armed with parchments that contained vital information about the amulet. They were determined to find the fourth and final piece before Camazotz could get ahold of it. But Camazotz needed those parchments, too, for they alone held the secret of where the fourth piece of the amulet could be found. Jack knew that the demon god would not be far behind them.

That had been five weeks ago. Since then, the friends

had traveled on a steamship, the *Bernadette*, as far as New Orleans, and then hired the *Providence* to take them to Puerto Morelos on the Yucatán coast. For that, they had used the last of the gold coins they had brought with them from Paris. The money was French and the schooner was American but, fortunately, gold was universal.

Jack glanced down from his perch and let his gaze sweep the deck. At the stern, he could see the *Providence*'s captain, Skip, at the wheel. He was tall and tanned from his many days at sea beneath the fierce southern sun. The friends had not gathered whether Skip was merely short for skipper, or the captain's name, or both. Other members of the crew were busy about the ship, coiling ropes or cleaning brass or doing any of the hundred and one things that were required to keep the schooner in good working order.

As Jack watched, Emily Cole came out of the deckhouse and made her way forward to join her brother, Ben, who sat at the base of the bowsprit, a sort of third mast that stuck out straight ahead of the boat. Ben was gazing out to sea thoughtfully. He was twelve, the same age as Jack, and dressed similarly in a linen shirt and canvas trousers. Only Ben's fair hair set the two boys apart. Jack wondered how Ben felt about returning to the Yucatán. He had been there before, on a scientific expedition that had been destroyed by the newly awoken Camazotz. Ben had lost his father, Harrison; his godfather, Edwin Sherwood; and his family's old friend Sir Donald Finlay to Camazotz and his vampires. For Ben, the Yucatán held terrible memories.

Jack sighed and turned his attention to the distant horizon. The sun and the endless sky seemed to fill him with light and air and hope. He couldn't help it—he whooped again.

Ben looked up as Emily approached along the slanting deck. He smiled as Jack's shout drifted down from above. "I see the ship's monkey is still happy," he remarked.

"*He* is," Emily agreed.

Ben moved up to make room for her. "You don't sound very cheerful, though," he added.

Emily was carefully clutching a piece of parchment, which she smoothed out on her lap as she sat down. It was covered with the strange hieroglyphs that Ben recognized as Mayan writing. He knew that Emily had been steadily translating the writing, bit by bit, until she had hit a stumbling block.

"Are they still giving you trouble?" he asked, referring to the hieroglyphs.

Emily nodded. "The writing changes just *here*," she said, indicating a break between two blocks of symbols. "It just *changes*," she repeated in frustration.

The ancient documents had belonged to a long-dead Spanish missionary named Sebastian Cabrillo, who had copied down the original Mayan hieroglyphics that described the pieces of the amulet and, hopefully, told where they were hidden. Emily had been making great progress in translating the glyphs, until suddenly—to her surprise—she had reached a passage where they just stopped making sense. The symbols were similar, but they seemed to be put together in a completely different way. The friends had been halfway across the Atlantic on the *Bernadette* at the time. Since then, Emily had spent hours every day on the problem to no avail.

And she was running out of time if they wanted to find the last piece of the amulet before Camazotz reached Mexico. They had been on the last steamship to leave France for America in a month. Camazotz could only follow by sail, but he could control the wind to speed a sailing boat on its way. At best, he would be a week behind them. At worst, no more than a few days.

"Don't give up, Emily," Ben said encouragingly. "You can decipher the symbols. I know you can."

"Thank you, Ben," she answered. Then she tore her eyes away from the parchment and looked up at the sun. "Well, at least we're prepared for the weather," she said brightly, obviously trying to change the subject.

"True," her brother replied.

Like Jack and Ben, Emily was dressed for Mexico's warm climate. She wore a white cotton blouse and a long cotton skirt with only one petticoat. Ben had talked her into this slightly unusual style of dress after seeing how comfortable Jack looked and remembering how he had sweltered in the jungle in his fashionable English tweed.

Just then, another happy shout echoed down from the mainmast. "Hey, I can see land! There's land ahead!"

"Well, it wasn't entirely unexpected." Skip laughed as he leaned on the roof of the deckhouse with a telescope to his eye. Jack, Ben, and Emily gathered around, straining their unaided eyes to see if they could spot the land themselves. From down on the deck it wasn't so easy.

"We are on course, and I pride myself on being a halfway decent navigator," Skip added, lowering the telescope and winking at Jack. "Still 'n' all, you got good eyes, son," he continued. His American accent still sounded odd to the three English children. "That there's Cape Catoche, the northeastern point of the Yucatán, right where it should be. Puts us about a hundred miles from Puerto Morelos. We gotta sail down the Yucatán Channel now, between the mainland and Cuba."

Skip glanced at the sun. It was nearing the horizon. Jack had learned to treat the sunset with great respect. Sunset was when the vampires came out. By day, they had to shelter undercover or wrap up well against the sun's rays. But at night, they were free to roam at will. The best thing about being in the middle of the ocean, Jack thought, was knowing that when the sun went down, the only thing he had to worry about was seeing in the dark.

"We'll sail through the night. Should raise Puerto

Morelos 'bout eight, nine o'clock in the morning if the wind holds." Skip folded up the telescope with a decisive snap, then looked shrewdly at his three passengers. "And your uncle's there waiting for you, right?"

"Right," Jack said innocently, looking him in the eye. He knew how Emily and Ben hated lying, but unfortunately, three people their age traveling alone drew attention. So, ever since they left Paris, they had been on their way to meet a fictitious relative who was always waiting just one step ahead of them.

Skip nodded and turned to go, then something caught his eye. He opened the telescope again and peered into the distance. "Say, someone's in a hurry."

The friends craned their necks to see what they could. Against the dark blur of the Yucatán on the horizon, they could just make out a white speck, drawing closer. It was the sails of another boat.

"Big boat, three masts . . ." Skip murmured with the telescope to his eye. "And in a stiff breeze like this, he's got way too much sail on. Taller the mast is, the more it bends and the quicker it breaks, but some people just can't be told."

"He's coming straight at us," Ben said thoughtfully. The three friends exchanged glances, and Jack knew they were all thinking the same thing: *Could it be Camazotz?*

But Jack knew it was unlikely. Camazotz was behind them; this boat was coming from the Yucatán. And the sun was still shining brightly. It would be difficult for vampires to sail a boat under those conditions.

7

Skip patted Ben on the shoulder. "Don't worry, son. By the time he gets here, assuming he holds that course, we'll be miles away. Sea's a big place, y'know." And with that, he went aft to talk to the sailor at the wheel, and the ship's cook popped his head up through the hatch to call the friends down to dinner.

A short staircase led down from the deckhouse into the main cabin. The cabin was lit from a skylight above and by oil lamps on the walls. The lamps and a central table were mounted in gimbals, metal rings that swung to keep the objects level as the boat pitched and swayed. Bunks were set into the walls along the sides of the cabin.

Dinner was a stew of chopped chicken and sausage with onions and garlic. It was hot and spicy and, Ben thought, utterly delicious. The cook called it gumbo.

The cook was serving out second helpings when Skip shouted, "Ready about!" from above.

The friends braced themselves. They knew Skip's command meant the ship was about to change direction. Still, it was an unusually sharp turn. The cook staggered and Ben's second helping of gumbo very nearly went in his lap.

"Hey, Skip, want to give us a chance next time?" the cook called up the stairs.

There was no response. Instead they all heard Skip shouting urgently, "Get the reefs out of the mainsail and break out the flying jib! Come on, move it!" And they heard the sound of the crew running to obey the captain's orders, their footsteps echoing on the deck overhead.

"Now, that don't sound good," the cook muttered. He quickly hung the stew pot in the galley and headed up on deck.

The friends looked at one another, and then they, too, headed for the stairs.

The boat they had seen earlier was much closer—no more than two hundred yards away now—and a bow wave of white water foamed before her. She was larger than the *Providence*, with three masts and square-rigged sails. But, Ben noticed, she looked tatty—her paint was peeling and her ropes and lines were frayed and slack. She made a very different sight from Skip's neat, well-maintained vessel.

Ben's eyes fell to the men lining the rail nearest the *Providence*. He realized with a chill that several of them carried rifles and a few held crossbows. A man in the bow was shouting instructions in Spanish across the gap of water.

"What's he saying?" Ben asked Emily. Her Spanish was much better than his.

"He wants us to drop our sails and let him come aboard," Emily replied.

Skip was at the wheel, keeping one eye on the other boat and one eye on the thrumming mainsail above him.

"Who are these men?" Ben called to him.

Skip looked down and saw the three friends for the first

time. "Now, you three get below, y'hear?" he shouted anxiously.

But Ben didn't move. "Who are these men?" he repeated.

"Are they pirates?" Emily asked nervously, not taking her gaze from the other vessel.

"Could be, ma'am, could be. Pirates used to be a frequent hazard in the Caribbean till your Royal Navy flushed 'em out. Never known 'em to come this far west, but there's a first time for everything. They don't mean us well, whoever they are."

"Can we outrun them?" Jack asked.

Skip snorted. "Little boat like us, son? Nuh-uh. We've only got two masts and two sails, while they can haul up more canvas just as they like. More canvas, more speed—that's how it goes. But we might be able to outmaneuver them. Ready about!"

He spun the wheel and the *Providence* turned her sharp prow into the wind. Overhead, the boom of the mainmast swung across the deck. The crew scrambled to haul in on the backstay, tightening the sail against the wind. Within a matter of seconds, the *Providence* was heading in a completely different direction, away from the stranger.

Ben glanced back at the other ship. She, too, was turning, but much more slowly. Her sailors were running around on deck, hauling in their own sails. Even from this distance, the crew didn't look as well organized as Skip's men.

"We're lighter, more maneuverable, and we can get

much closer to the wind than they can," Skip said. "On the other hand, they're just plain faster than us, so it kind of evens out. Now, I gave y'all an order to get below. You're underfoot and, besides, there might be fighting."

"We can fight!" Jack told him.

Skip smiled grimly. "Sure, son. I bet you're real handy with your fists, but these guys have guns. Now for the last time, get yourselves below, 'fore I have you carried down."

The three friends reluctantly ducked back down into the cabin. They tried to follow what was going on above by listening to the sounds from the deck. The *Providence* lurched again several times, zigzagging her way across the Gulf as Skip tried to shake off their pursuers.

Then all three friends jumped as they heard a muffled *boom*, followed immediately by the hiss and crack of something flying through the air not far overhead. Startled shouts echoed down from the deck above.

Ben stood on tiptoes to peer out of the skylight. He only caught a glimpse of the other boat, now very close indeed, but it was enough. He could see the cannon mounted on a swivel in the other ship's bow. "That was a warning shot!" he exclaimed. "They've got a cannon on deck. The *Providence* can't outrun a cannonball."

And sure enough, the *Providence* was slowing down. Up above, the crewmen were hauling in the sails. Within moments, the larger boat was drawing alongside. A shadow fell across the skylight and the cabin darkened as the other boat moved in.

Footsteps thumped on the deck above as men jumped aboard from the larger vessel. The friends looked at one another.

"It can't be Camazotz, can it?" Emily asked nervously.

Ben considered the possibility for a moment. They had all been so sure Camazotz was behind them—but could he just *possibly* have gotten ahead? Then he dismissed the notion. Camazotz would not come for them in sunlight.

"I really think it's only pirates," he said, and frustration welled up inside him. Had they really come this far, fought evil creatures from the depths of hell, and risked their lives only to be thwarted by a bunch of violent, greedy sea thieves?

Up on deck, a harsh voice was shouting orders in Spanish. Then footsteps sounded on the stairs, and a man entered the cabin. He was dressed like a sailor, but he carried a pistol in one hand and some kind of spear in the other. He cast an eye over the three friends and shouted back up the stairs. Other men appeared behind him. All of them had dark hair and flat faces.

Ben frowned. He had seen faces like this before. "They look Mayan," he whispered, "not Mexican."

"*No mueva. Quede allá,*" the first man ordered.

"He said: 'Don't move. Stay where you are,'" Emily said quietly. One of the other men had pulled out his gun and was pointing it at them. The message was clear, even without Emily's translation.

The first man moved past them to search the ship. He

held the spear in front of himself defensively. Ben wondered why he chose to rely on the spear when he also carried a gun.

Once the man had satisfied himself that there was nobody else on board, he came back and looked thoughtfully at Ben, Emily, and Jack. Then he grasped his spear firmly in both hands and began to advance.

Ben and Jack immediately stepped in front of Emily. Ben was frantically casting his eyes around the cabin for something he could use as a weapon.

"Hold!" came a sharp command in English from the stairs. "Leave them be."

Ben stopped looking for a weapon and turned his attention to the newcomer. Something about his voice was familiar.

The man with the spear stepped back obediently as the newcomer entered the cabin. Light from the skylight fell on his face, and Ben felt his jaw drop as he stared in shock and disbelief.

Standing in front of him, slightly thinner and grayer than Ben remembered, but nevertheless very much alive, was a man who Ben had been certain was dead. His father's best friend and his own godfather, the man who had sacrificed himself to Camazotz so that Harrison and Ben might escape the vampires. Edwin Sherwood now confronted his godson, with a loaded crossbow trained on Ben's heart.

CHAPTER TWO

"Uncle Edwin!" Emily breathed in amazement.

"Uncle Edwin?" Jack said. "I thought he was supposed to be dead!"

Jack had heard all about Edwin Sherwood from Ben and Emily. He wasn't their uncle but their godfather, and had been their father's best friend and colleague. The two men had often traveled together on expeditions, never happier than when they were crawling through the ruins of an ancient civilization. On the original, fateful expedition to Mexico, Edwin and Harrison had realized that their friend Sir Donald was possessed by the Mayan demon god Camazotz, and they had chosen to confront him together. Unfortunately the two Englishmen were no match for a god and his small army of vampires. Eventually Edwin had stayed to fight so that Harrison could escape and save Ben.

Jack knew Ben had believed Edwin to be dead—another victim of the vampire plague. But now, suddenly, that had changed.

"Uncle . . . Edwin . . ." Ben said slowly. He and Emily couldn't take their eyes off the man.

But Edwin's expression was grim. "Take them up on deck," he commanded. "Now!"

And the next moment, the three friends found themselves being marched out of the cabin.

They blinked as they emerged into the sunlight. Jack saw that the two boats had been lashed together. The rail of the larger one was lined with armed men, while Skip and the rest of the *Providence*'s crew sat under guard on the deck of their own ship.

"Uncle Edwin," Ben began, "what are—"

"Don't talk to me!" Edwin snapped. "Just face the sun. Look at it!"

Jack, Ben, and Emily stood in a row and looked out over the sea, hands up over their eyes to shield the glare as they stood bathed in sunlight. Their captors seemed to be expecting something to happen.

Eventually one of Edwin's companions said, "I think they are human, señor."

"Well, yes," Jack agreed.

Edwin just grinned. He came forward and grasped Ben by the shoulders. "Ben, you really are alive!" he exclaimed.

Ben beamed up at him. "I certainly am."

Edwin finally seemed to notice who Ben was with. "And Emily! What on earth are you doing here?"

He pulled them both into a laughing, three-way hug.

After a moment, Ben pulled away and turned toward his friend. "Uncle, this is Jack Harkett," he said.

Jack had been waiting to one side, not sure if he was still under guard or not.

Edwin looked at him. "Pleased to meet you," he said. "And how do you know these two?"

"Well," said Jack, "it's kind of a long story—"

"Señor!" They were interrupted by one of Edwin's men, who had emerged from the main cabin holding the ancient parchments in his hand.

"Oh, be careful with those!" Emily said anxiously.

The man spoke to Edwin in rapid Spanish. Edwin's eyebrows rose. "Do you know what these are?" he asked. "Felipe tells me they contain the ancient writing of the priests of Chac."

"Well, yes," Ben put in. "That's why we're here."

"I'm hoping these parchments will tell us where to find the last piece of an amulet that Camazotz badly wants," Emily explained. She turned to the man holding the documents. "Please let me take them," she said. And reluctantly he handed them over.

"You remember Camazotz?" Ben asked.

Edwin gave a short, grim laugh. "Yes, Ben, I can safely say I remember Camazotz."

"Well, he'll be about a week behind us," said Ben. "He's on our track, but we took a steamship from Paris, and he missed it, so he would have had to sail."

"*Paris?* What was Camazotz doing in . . . ?" Edwin gave up with a sigh. "I can see we've got a great deal to catch up on. We were patrolling these waters, on the lookout for

Camazotz, but if you're sure he's about a week behind you, we can afford to change our plans. You'd better come across to our boat." Edwin turned away and began calling orders to his men.

Jack watched their captors tuck away their guns and run to their lines, ready to cast off.

"Hey, mister!" No longer held at gunpoint, Skip came striding angrily down the deck toward them. He stopped when he was almost nose to nose with Edwin. "Just what the heck is going on? I should report you to the United States Navy. They're none too keen on pirates!"

"We're not pirates, sir," Edwin responded flatly. "If we were, you'd be at the bottom of the Gulf by now."

Skip drew breath for an angry retort.

"Look, Skip," Emily interrupted quickly. "They've put their guns away, and they're leaving. And we're going with them—of our own free will. I promise you, we're in no danger."

Skip looked unconvinced. "Well, if you say so."

"We do. And thank you for bringing us this far." Emily stood on tiptoes and gave him a kiss on the cheek. Then she turned to the side of the boat so that Edwin could help her across to the larger vessel.

Ben shook hands with Skip. "Thanks, Skip," he said, and followed his sister.

Jack was the last to go. He gave Skip his most winning smile as they shook hands. "Told you their uncle was waiting for them," he said brightly.

As the two ships pulled apart, Jack saw the crew of the *Providence* hauling up the sails. The schooner turned away to the north, heading back to New Orleans.

"I know you were going to Puerto Morelos," Edwin said as the larger boat set off westward to sail along the Yucatán's north shore, "but I want to take you to our base camp, and this is a more direct route."

They stood in a circle on the foredeck and looked at one another.

"So," Edwin asked, "who's going to tell their story first?"

"You," said Ben at once. "You were supposed to be dead! Father said you were overpowered by vampires when you confronted Camazotz. He said . . ." Ben's voice shook and he stopped, momentarily overcome by his memories.

Jack thought of everything Ben had told him about his escape from the Yucatán—his lonely trek out of the jungle after his father had died, and his terrible voyage back to England as a stowaway on a sailing ship full of vampires. How much easier would it have been if Ben had known Edwin was still alive to help him?

But if Ben had had it any easier, Jack reflected, he wouldn't be as determined or resistant as he was now. And he might never have met Jack.

"Well, we certainly confronted Camazotz," Edwin

agreed, "and he set his creatures on us. I passed out as two of them bit into my neck." He pulled down his collar. The scars from two distinct sets of bite marks showed clearly on his neck, pearly white against his tanned skin. "And then I woke up to find I had been rescued by the Brotherhood. They had discovered the empty cave where they knew Camazotz ought to be, and they followed our trail through the jungle. They finally caught up in time to see me being attacked by vampires. They charged and chased the creatures off."

"And who are the Brotherhood?" asked Emily.

"*They* are," Edwin said, waving a hand around to indicate the boat and the other men on board. "The Brotherhood of Chac. Chac was—"

"The Mayan lightning god," Jack put in eagerly. "And Camazotz's enemy."

"That's right." Edwin lowered his voice. "And the Brotherhood has been watching and waiting for Camazotz's return for a thousand years, ever since he was banished. They knew he would reawaken, and the knowledge has been passed from father to son for centuries. When they found the empty cave, they knew the time had come."

"If they knew Camazotz was in the cave," Ben said, "why didn't they just block it up? Or try to destroy him once and for all?"

"Camazotz was banished there by magic," Edwin answered gravely. "It wasn't just walls of rock that held him. He was bound by forces far more mysterious than that. He couldn't get out for one thousand years. But through all those centuries, no mortal man could touch him. Camazotz is a god. It is no easy matter for men to destroy a god. The Brotherhood did what they could. They carved the full story of Camazotz on the rocks around the cave mouth, and they planted the whole area with blood rose. The blood rose is a plant—"

"We know," Ben interrupted. "It's poisonous to vampires. It has very sharp thorns."

"That cut you if you so much as look at them," Jack added with feeling.

"And its fragrance is overpowering," put in Emily.

Edwin nodded, looking slightly taken aback. Jack could tell he was surprised by how much the three friends knew.

Edwin pointed to one of the men. "You see the spear he's carrying? It has blood rose wrapped around the tip, making it a very useful weapon against vampires. In the days when Camazotz was worshipped, the plant was burned on sight. The hieroglyphs of the time always show it preceded with the symbol for flame. Camazotz wanted it destroyed wherever it was found. He wanted the Yucatán free of the blood rose. Fortunately it's a very persistent plant."

"What happened after the Brotherhood found you?" Emily asked.

"I was unconscious for a whole day. When I came to, I told everything to the Brotherhood's chieftain, a man named Abran. I asked him to look for you, Ben, and for Harrison.

He found your father's body and I saw to it that Harrison had a proper Christian burial. But there was no sign of you, though we searched high and low. Some of the locals in Puerto Morelos said they saw a boy of your description hanging around a ship on the quay. They also saw Camazotz board the ship just before it set sail. I reckoned that even if you were alive when you went on board, you wouldn't have been for much longer."

"I hid in the cable locker for the entire voyage," Ben muttered. "Everyone else—everyone else *human*—died."

Jack remembered watching the ghost ship sailing up the Thames at sunset. It was at the end of its long journey from Mexico. He had met Ben very shortly afterward, half starved from being in hiding so long with very little food. "That's why you dragged us into the sun, isn't it?" he said thoughtfully. "Just in case."

Edwin nodded. "The moment I saw you again today, Ben, I could only think that you must be a vampire. I'm sorry."

Ben shrugged. "I understand."

Edwin continued, "There's not much more to tell. After we couldn't find you, well, we knew Camazotz had awoken, and Abran suspected he would return to the Yucatán before too long. He asked if I would join the Brotherhood, add my weight to the battle. But I was worried that Camazotz would wreak havoc in Britain. I tried to warn the British authorities. Puerto Morelos doesn't rank a consul—much too small—but I found a British official in Mérida. The man

21

plainly thought I was crazy. So I decided to accept Abran's offer. He assured me Camazotz would come back here eventually. I've been hoping it would be within my lifetime.

"The Brotherhood has been arming itself against Camazotz, preparing for his return. Recently we've seen the vampires becoming agitated. They can sense their master's presence, and they could feel that he was on his way back. So we acquired this ship and we've been patrolling the coast ever since."

"So there are still vampires in Mexico?" Jack said. "I thought they all went with Camazotz."

"We thought so, too, but it soon became obvious that wasn't the case. Abran decided Camazotz must have taken most of them but left some behind to start recruiting in preparation for his return. We kill as many as we can, but still their numbers grow every day." Edwin shook his head grimly, then turned to Ben. "Now, tell me what you three have been up to."

So Ben told Edwin about his hellish journey from Mexico to England, about the battle that he, Jack, and Emily had fought against Camazotz, and about how they had eventually succeeded in driving the vampires out of London. He went on to explain how they had found themselves forced to fight Camazotz again in Paris, how they learned of the amulet, and how their quest for the final piece of the amulet had brought them to Mexico. "Unfortunately," Ben finished with a sigh, "we don't know exactly *where* the final piece is hidden. Emily's having trouble translating the information on the parchments."

Edwin smiled for the first time since Ben began his tale when he heard this. "Well, I'm taking you to meet the rest of the Brotherhood and someone who might be able to help with your translation," he said. "Her name's Lorena, and she's an expert in the ancient hieroglyphs. She'll want to see your parchments. We've learned a lot from the inscriptions around Camazotz's cave — but what you have in these parchments is invaluable."

"Are there many people in the Brotherhood of Chac?" Jack inquired.

"About fifty or so," Edwin replied.

Jack whistled, and the three friends looked at one another. They were used to fighting Camazotz alone, Jack thought, and it was strange to discover that so many others were fighting against him, too. But it was marvelous to feel they weren't on their own anymore.

They sailed through the night along the north coast of the Yucatán. Jack had yet to see any more of the peninsula than a low blur on the horizon. But now he could smell it.

When the first scents reached his nostrils, he knew they hadn't come from the sea. The breeze was blowing out of the interior, and it was warm and musty. It was air that came from the jungles Ben had told him about — where the sun never reached the ground, where the air was saturated with moisture, and where every surface was clammy with the jungle's sweat.

They dropped anchor the next morning, and when he came up on deck, Jack got his first real glimpse of the Yucatán. Bluffs of white-yellow limestone, softened and worn by the sea, rose out of the water a hundred yards away. Waves dashed against the cliffs, then fell away with sucks and gurgles.

Ben and Emily were already up, talking to their godfather.

"Where are we?" asked Emily.

"Eighty, ninety miles west of Cape Catoche," Edwin answered. "About a day's journey from the camp, and about two days' journey from Camazotz's cave."

Jack listened with interest. The cave was where it had all started. Camazotz had been banished there for a thousand years—a thousand years ago. He had awoken just in time to take advantage of Sir Donald's expedition and return with it to civilization. Jack wondered if he would get a chance to see the cave for himself.

The ship's skiff was being lowered into the water. It splashed down and a rope ladder was dropped after it, unfurling as it fell. Edwin climbed down first so that he could help the others from below. Jack's practice in the rigging paid off, and he scrambled down quickly with no help. Emily and Ben were a little more cautious, but soon they were all safely seated in the little boat. A couple of crew-men joined them and they cast off from the ship's side.

The crewmen rowed with one oar each. Powerful strokes carried the skiff toward the cliffs. Edwin sat in the stern, guiding the little boat, while Jack sat in the bow, eagerly watching the bluff approach. As far as he could see, the skiff was heading straight for the rocks. But then he noticed a small fissure, a natural crack hidden by the rough contours of the cliff face. The skiff passed quickly into the narrow channel, and the waves surged in with it, carrying the boat the last few feet so that it burst out into a small, almost cir-cular cove. A couple more pulls on the oars, and the bow crunched gently on a white sandy beach.

The friends threw their boots and socks out onto the sand and then jumped out of the boat and splashed through the sea to the shore. Then Edwin and Jack gave the boat a good shove back into the water, and the two crewmen rowed it back toward the channel in the rock.

Ben was watching the water surge around his feet. Jack noticed the pensive expression on his face and put a hand on his shoulder.

"It's going to be different this time, mate," he said softly.

Ben looked up at him and smiled back. "I know," he replied. "This time, we're going to win!"

CHAPTER THREE

"Señor!" The shout echoed around the small cove. Jack looked up to see a small path winding up the rock face at one end of the beach. A man stood at the top, waving.

Edwin waved back. "Boots on," he said. "We need to get moving."

They climbed up the path to meet the man who had waved at them. He was young—in his twenties, Jack guessed—and tall, with an infectious grin. He had a flat, Mayan face but dark, wavy hair that also hinted of Spanish blood. Behind him was a small collection of huts, where four other men were packing up provisions.

The man was obviously surprised to see three strangers with Edwin. *"Señor Sherwood, quiénes son sus amigos?"*

"Roberto is one of the Brotherhood's captains," Edwin said. He turned to Roberto and explained the situation quickly in Spanish. The other men of the Brotherhood gathered around to listen, and when Edwin mentioned the parchments there was a murmur of excitement.

"We must show them to Lorena," said Roberto in English that was inflected with a strong Spanish accent.

Edwin nodded and Roberto hurried away, shouting orders in Spanish.

"Going to be a long walk," Jack remarked. He remembered that Edwin had said they were a day's journey from the camp. But after so long at sea, he looked forward to stretching his legs.

"Not for us," Edwin said with a smile. "Our transport," he added, gesturing toward a small enclosure.

Jack looked where he was pointing. "Funny-looking horses!" he exclaimed. The animals were oddly misshapen— a far cry from the fine creatures that the three friends were accustomed to seeing in the streets of London and Paris. These were no more than five feet high and covered with rough gray hair. Their ears were longer than a horse's usually were, too.

"Mules, señor!" Roberto told him as he returned, leading two of the animals. "A donkey father and a horse mother. They are strong and will carry you forever."

"Mules. Right," Jack said. He eyed them warily. In Jack's opinion, any animal larger than a cat was to be avoided. These had minds of their own, but you were expected to sit on them. He thought it sounded like a risky combination. He looked at his mule suspiciously as he approached it. The mule looked back without enthusiasm.

Roberto showed Jack how to sit on the saddle. It was padded leather, but Jack could feel the animal's sharp backbone underneath him. Everyone else was saddling up as well.

"Is everyone coming, then?" Jack asked curiously. "Didn't know we got an escort."

Roberto looked at him gravely. "The jungle is not as safe as it once was, señor. We take no chances."

And Jack brooded on that thought as they set off into the interior of the Yucatán.

The land was low and scrubby, the soil dry and sandy, and everything was covered by a kind of spiky grass that seemed to grow no higher than a man's knee. Jack felt uncomfortably exposed on the back of his mule. Even in the middle of the ocean, he had been surrounded by the ship—a man-made object and a sort of little city to replace the big city he had grown up in. But here, about the only man-made things for miles around were the clothes he and the others wore. Everything else was *natural*, and Jack didn't trust it.

As they moved away from the coast, the sea breeze died and the temperature began to rise. Hot, humid air drifted around Jack's face, and sweat made his clothes cling to his skin. He shook his damp hair out of his eyes, and heavy drops of sweat ran down his face. He began to wish he had had his hair cut shorter.

The grass gradually grew higher and trees began to appear. Jack was talking to Roberto, telling him about London, when he suddenly realized that the path through the scrub had become a track through a forest. Branches stretched overhead. They had entered the jungle.

The mules carried them slowly along a beaten track through the trees for some hours. And then, suddenly, the path opened out into a clearing about fifty feet across. Jack looked up at the clear blue sky above. He had lost track of time, but going by the emptiness of his stomach he guessed it was well into the afternoon.

"We'll stop for lunch," Edwin said. "Take care getting down."

Jack looked down and recoiled, almost falling out of his saddle. It wasn't a clearing after all. The ground to the mule's right fell away in a sheer drop of a hundred feet or more. The mule turned its head to look at him, and Jack was sure he detected a mocking gleam in its placid eyes. He glared back at it, then carefully climbed down to the ground on the mule's left-hand side.

He winced and stretched. As well as losing track of time, he seemed to have lost all sense of feeling in the lower half of his body. It was good to get the blood flowing again.

Ben and Emily carefully dismounted, then edged over to the sheer drop and peered down into the chasm.

Roberto said something that sounded to Jack like, "Say nohtay."

"Er, pardon?" Jack asked, puzzled, as he went over to join his friends.

Ben grinned. "He said *cenote*, Jack. It's the word for one of these holes."

"The Spanish took it from the Mayan word *dznot*," put in Edwin. "It means . . ."

"Big hole in the ground?" Jack hazarded a guess.

"Big hole in the ground, with water at the bottom," Edwin confirmed.

They all craned their necks to look down into the depths. The walls seemed to be sheer, craggy limestone. At the bottom, Jack could just make out a pool of water—crystal clear and a deep, rich blue.

"There are no rivers in the Yucatán," Edwin explained, "but the limestone is riddled with holes like this, probably eroded over thousands of years. Many of them lead to great labyrinths of caverns that no one has ever explored. The Mayans relied on them for water. They also associated them with their gods, so the *cenotes* were used for sacrifice, human and otherwise. The records say they would throw in offerings—gold statues and the like. Harrison used to think that if we could just get someone to dive into one of the pools, we'd retrieve some real treasures."

Jack decided he would happily do without the treasures if it meant he didn't have to venture down one of the water holes. It didn't look very inviting.

After a simple lunch of dried meat and water, the little party climbed back onto the mules and continued into the jungle. The trees towered above them again, their leafy branches cutting out most of the sunlight. Jack thought of the vampires that might be lurking in the shadowy jungle depths and shuddered.

Think of a church. Now imagine the air inside it to be very, very hot and heavy and humid. The windows and

30

the floor are covered with rotting leaves, so there is a stench of decaying vegetation and no light. (Even at midday, we sometimes have to light a lamp.) Imagine the pillars are trees, not in two neat rows down the aisle but everywhere. And they are thickly wrapped in vines and ivy and every kind of climbing plant, because everything wants to get up above the tree canopy and reach the sunlight. You are beginning to get a feel for the Yucatán jungle.

Emily remembered those words perfectly. Ben had written them for her in his journal on his first visit to Mexico. They had both been bitterly disappointed when she had fallen ill just as the expedition was due to leave London. She had had to stay behind in the care of their housekeeper, Mrs. Mills, but her brother had promised to keep a journal for her, a record of all his experiences.

In fact, Emily reflected, Ben's journal had contained much more than either of them had expected. He had recounted the whole terrible story of how the expedition had encountered Camazotz. But he had also described the jungle, and now Emily was experiencing it for herself.

The first thing she noticed was the concert of different noises, interconnected and tangled, like the plants around them. Small insects and unseen mammals rustled and crashed through the undergrowth, creating a sea of sound that rose and fell all around her.

And the scents and smells fascinated Emily. Damp was always there, a rich tang that lingered because water

31

was everywhere, either falling from the sky or evaporating from the leaves and trees in the hot Mexican sun. But there was also the smell of new green buds and of decaying vegetation, the sweet fragrance of flowers in bloom and the musky animal smell of the mules.

And then a particular aroma reached her nostrils—one that Emily recognized immediately. She saw Ben and Jack stiffen in their saddles as they, too, smelled it.

It was a faint, sweet perfume at this distance, but Emily knew how heavy and overwhelming it would become as they drew closer. "That's blood rose," she said.

"Lots of it," Jack agreed.

"We're near the camp," Edwin told them.

The track brought them out of the trees and into a clearing. Jack glanced quickly at the ground to check that it really was a clearing and not another *cenote*, but he needn't have worried. This was much wider than the water hole had been, and the ground was littered with tree stumps. Obviously this clearing had been deliberately cut out of the jungle.

Ahead was a tall hedge of blood rose. The leaves were a very dark green, as if the plant was deliberately trying to set off the flowers, which were a bright, rich red—vivid as fresh blood, and unmistakable.

As he drew closer, Jack could make out the thorns he

remembered so well. They were sharp and curved, like the teeth of the vampires the plant could destroy, and they had saved his life on several occasions. Jack felt a strange affection for the plant.

A wooden watchtower stood at one corner of the hedge, its sides festooned with roses. There were men up there who called down to the ground in Spanish when they saw Edwin and his party arrive. A section of the hedge swung out, and Jack saw that it was a normal wooden gate that had been garlanded with blood rose. Through the gate he could see two rows of huts set on low stilts and surrounded by a jumble of other huts and tents. This was the headquarters of the Brotherhood of Chac.

"It's like a fortress," Ben commented.

"A fortress designed against one specific enemy," said Edwin. "Everything is defended against vampires. As you can see, there's a plentiful supply of blood rose and every building has at least one person who sleeps there at night, to make it a home. No vampires can get in without an invitation."

"It don't look a thousand years old, though," Jack remarked.

"Oh, it's not," agreed Edwin. "It's brand-new. The Brotherhood never needed a headquarters while Camazotz was confined to his cave. Now that he's free, the Brotherhood has a great deal of work to do, so Abran decided they needed a proper camp. There was a natural cluster of blood rose in this area, there's a *cenote* nearby for water, and we're right on the edge of Camazotz's traditional territory. This seemed the best place to be."

"How far away is the cave?" Ben asked.

"Another day's ride." Edwin pointed down the trail, past the camp and back into the trees. "That way."

They rode through the gate and into the camp. Roberto and his men were greeted by other members of the Brotherhood, while the friends drew some curious looks. They gratefully climbed down from the mules and Roberto led the creatures off to a corral on the camp's far side to be fed and watered.

Ben stretched his aching muscles and groaned.

Edwin smiled. "You get used to it," he said.

"Señor Sherwood!" came a man's voice.

Edwin's face brightened. "Abran!" he exclaimed, and turned to meet his friend.

A man and a woman were approaching from the largest of the wooden huts. Jack noticed that the two newcomers were like all the other members of the Brotherhood he had seen so far—more Mayan than Mexican. Abran's short-cut hair was graying and his somber face was wrinkled. He wore a long robe that looked as if it had once been grand, though it was now somewhat frayed and faded, and he did not walk so much as prowl like a cat, Jack thought. The man was a natural predator, aware of everything and every-one around him, and the other members of the Brotherhood eyed him with respect, standing a little straighter as he stalked past.

The woman by his side was short and round, with twinkling brown eyes and a ready smile on her face. She had long, dark hair, which she had drawn back into a ponytail tied with a bright orange ribbon. Her clothes were colorful and flowing, and her whole being seemed to radiate good cheer. Where Abran prowled, she bustled.

"*Edwin, esto es inesperado!*" she said.

Jack and Ben both looked hopefully at Emily, who rolled her eyes. "She said, 'This is unexpected,'" she whispered.

Edwin started to speak in rapid Spanish to the pair.

After a few moments, Abran held up a hand to stop him. "Friends from England?" he said. "Then as a courtesy to our guests we will speak in English."

"Yes, of course," the woman added warmly. "That will make them feel more welcome. My name is Lorena and I am delighted to meet you. We have never had such young visitors. You must all be tired after your journey."

"Indeed." Abran bowed solemnly. "I am Abran, chieftain of the Brotherhood of Chac. My ancestors have carried this responsibility, passing it from father to son, for the last thousand years. I am the forty-seventh to watch for the return of He Who Walks By Darkness. I bid you welcome."

He said it with such finality that Jack got the impression he didn't invite casual conversation.

Abran looked sternly at Edwin. "I say this because I

know there must be a good reason for one of my trusted lieutenants to bring three children to this place!"

Edwin simply smiled. "Abran, let me introduce Emily Cole, Ben Cole, and Jack Harkett."

Abran looked surprised. "Ben Cole?" he asked. "Is that . . ."

"Yes," Edwin said with a grin. "*That* Ben Cole. The son of Harrison, the boy I thought was dead."

Abran bowed to Ben. "Then it is a pleasure and an honor to meet you."

Ben flushed. Jack guessed he was unused to being famous.

"Wait until you see what Emily has brought you, Lorena," Edwin continued.

Emily opened up her bag and handed the parchments over to Lorena, who stared at them in utter amazement.

"Oh, my goodness! Oh, señorita! Have you any idea what is on these?" she asked eagerly.

"Well," Emily said, sounding a trifle bashful. She handed over the notebook that she used for her translations. "I do know some of it. You see, I used my father's notes to translate as far as I could."

Lorena was still holding the parchments and didn't have a hand to spare for the notebook. "Show me the first page," she instructed breathlessly. So Emily opened the notebook, and Lorena compared Emily's notes with the first parchment. "It is almost perfect!" she exclaimed at last.

She gave Emily a delighted smile. "Oh, you have no idea how glad I am to see you! You must show me everything you have done right away."

"Well, I ran into a problem," Emily began.

"Never mind, never mind, I expect we can solve it together. Now, come—"

"One moment!" Abran interrupted. "These two are the children of Harrison Cole. Sherwood, you should show them . . ."

Edwin slapped his forehead. "Of course," he said, and turned to face the three friends. "Come with me."

Jack had no idea where they were going, and he could see from their expressions that Ben and Emily were equally bewildered. But they followed Edwin obediently.

At the edge of the camp, near the hedge, was a small, fenced-off area. Inside it were several mounds of earth, each with a wooden cross at its head. On one of the crosses were the words:

HERE LIE THE MORTAL REMAINS

OF HARRISON COLE

BELOVED FATHER OF EMILY AND BENEDICT

DIED 3RD APRIL 1850

"I told you I saw to it that he had a decent burial," Edwin said quietly.

Emily and Ben were staring at the cross, lost for words.

Edwin patted Ben on the shoulder. "We'll leave you alone," he said quietly. "Come on, Jack." And with that, Edwin and Jack headed back to the main camp together.

Jack glanced over his shoulder once. Ben and Emily were kneeling by their father's grave, their arms around each other.

Jack had never known his parents. Once, he had envied his friends for having had a family. He didn't envy them their grief.

"Jack, I'll leave you with Lorena for a moment," said Edwin when they were back at the huts. "There are a few things I have to take care of." He gave a friendly wave and walked off.

Lorena smiled. "Come, Jack," she said, waving the parchments. "Perhaps you can help me, too."

"I doubt that," Jack muttered, but he followed her into her hut.

It was a single room, small and square, but the windows and door were wide open and it was as airy as possible for the middle of the jungle. At one end there was a bedroll set up on a small platform. At the other was a desk and a chair, surrounded by bookshelves and piles of paper.

"I know Emily has other things on her mind," Lorena said brightly. "So perhaps you can tell me where these came from?"

"Oh, I can do *that*," Jack said, feeling relieved. He told her what he knew. The first few parchments had come from the British Museum in London. Professor Adensnap had produced them when they had all met for the first time. The missionary Sebastian Cabrillo had copied the hieroglyphs down centuries ago, adding his own comments in Spanish here and there.

In Paris, the Vicomte de Montargis had shown the friends some more parchments. They had obviously been written by Sebastian Cabrillo, and from them the friends had learned more about Camazotz—but still not enough.

"Marvelous!" Lorena enthused, clapping her hands when Jack had finished. "This is marvelous. You three coming here with these parchments is the best thing that could have happened. And—"

Just then, there was a knock at the open door to the hut. Jack and Lorena turned to see Emily and Ben standing there, peering inside.

"Emily!" Lorena bustled over and drew Emily toward the table. "Just the person I needed to see. Dear Jack was just explaining to me . . ."

Within seconds, Lorena and Emily were poring over the manuscripts, chatting happily together.

Ben wandered over to join Jack.

"Um . . . how are you?" Jack asked cautiously.

Ben smiled grimly. "Even more determined than ever to defeat Camazotz once and for all. I'd already said my good-byes to my father, remember? But I'm glad Em got the chance." He glanced over to where Emily and Lorena were conferring. "More translating, I see."

"Yup," Jack agreed. "There's two of 'em now. We didn't know when we was well off."

Emily's work on the parchments had been invaluable to them in the past. Both boys knew it. But they also knew that it was immensely boring waiting for her to come up with something useful.

"Ah, boys! There you are." Edwin had come in, followed by Roberto.

"*Shh!*" Lorena and Emily hissed together from across the hut.

Edwin tried again. "Ah, boys," he whispered. "We've found something for you to do. Come along with us."

Jack and Ben walked out into the sunlight and followed Edwin and Roberto across the center of the camp.

"Abran thinks—and I agree—that if you two are to join us, you should have some proper training. He says this is not a place for boys who cannot fight—"

"Can't fight?" Ben exclaimed indignantly.

"Does he know what we did to Camazotz in London?" Jack demanded.

"Yes, yes, I stand corrected!" Edwin laughed. "I know you have both fought vampires before."

"But this is the jungle," put in Roberto. "It is very different from the city. We have lived in the jungle all our lives. It is important that you learn our ways."

"A man would be a fool not to learn from these people," Edwin said seriously. "This way."

The smell of blood rose was everywhere in the camp, but it got stronger as they approached a busy group of men and women in a corner of the clearing. As they got closer, Jack noticed that a pile of cut blood-rose stems lay in the center, and all around it the men and women were making arrows, slinging strings to bows, and creating the blood-rose spears Ben and Jack had seen before.

"This is the armory," said Roberto proudly. "This is where we prepare for war against Camazotz."

"And we need as many hands as we can get," Edwin told them. "Ben, you can work with me. Roberto, could you take Jack with you?"

"Of course," said Roberto readily, and he led Jack over to a pile of sharpened staves and showed him how to tie the blood rose to the staves with twine. Suddenly what had been a simple length of wood had become an effective weapon against a vampire—and it was long enough that the holder could keep a safe distance away from the creature's teeth and claws.

Jack had fought vampires with blood rose before, but only with a branch that he had held in his bare hands. The thorns had scratched and torn his skin and he had been forced to get very close to the enemy to use the branch. Spears were an excellent idea, he thought approvingly, wondering why the idea hadn't occurred to him back in London.

A short distance away, he saw Ben cutting notches into the tips of arrows while Edwin carefully plucked the thorns off sprigs of blood rose and squeezed them into the notches to create arrowheads. Another excellent idea, Jack thought—blood rose delivered from a distance. Now he understood why some of the crewmen on Edwin's ship carried crossbows.

"Thought we was going to do some training," he said to Roberto after a while.

"We will train you," Roberto agreed. "But to master your weapon, you must first understand how it is made."

"And does everyone help make these?" Jack asked.

Roberto nodded. "It is our honor to serve the Brotherhood," he said cheerfully. He lifted the spear he had just made, hefting it in one hand to feel its balance. "I grew up doing this. I have always known that one day I might have the privilege of doing battle with He Who Walks By Darkness."

"Believe me, it ain't much of a privilege," Jack muttered as he tugged the twine firmly around a wooden shaft, binding a sprig of blood rose into place.

"But it is, Jack! And there are many secrets we can teach you. Secrets born of ancient knowledge handed down through the centuries. The hidden ways of the jungle. The plants that will kill and the plants that will cure. The rituals, such as the chant to protect the mind from the Evil One's control . . ."

"What's that?" Jack asked, perking up suddenly. He laid down his spear.

"The chant," said Roberto. "The Evil One has the power to control the minds of men. He can make them do what they would not do."

"Yeah, don't I know it," said Jack. He, Ben, and Emily had all experienced Camazotz's mind control. The demon god had gotten inside their heads and forced them to lay down their weapons. "We could have done with that chant," Jack said with feeling.

"Well, it is very simple," Roberto told him. "*Lah yich saknik, maknik Chac.* It calls upon the light of Chac to banish the darkness of Camazotz from the mind."

"*Lah meek Chacnik . . .*" Jack repeated hesitantly.

"*Lah yich saknik . . .*" Roberto corrected.

"*Lah* yich *Chacnik . . .*"

"*Saknik . . .*"

"*Saknik, maknik Chac . . .*" Eventually Jack had it. He found that there was a certain rhythm to the words. "*Lah yich saknik, maknik Chac,*" he chanted happily.

"Perfect," Roberto said with a smile.

Jack grinned back and picked up another sprig of blood rose. A thin line of red blood suddenly welled up on the back of his hand. The thorns had scratched him, but they were so sharp he had hardly felt it. He smiled at Ben and held his hand up. "Just like old times, ain't it?" he said.

43

CHAPTER FOUR

"The legendary amulet of Camazotz," said Lorena slowly. She shook her head and straightened up from the parchments. "Well, well. We have heard of it, of course, but as we never found any of the parts, we assumed it was just a myth."

"Camazotz took one part with him into the cave," Emily told her. "And two of the other three sections were found by Europeans."

"So the fourth piece is still hidden somewhere in the Yucatán," Lorena said thoughtfully. She tapped the parchments. "We must find it, Emily. If Camazotz were to have all four pieces, it would be a catastrophe."

"Do you know what the amulet can do?" Emily asked. "We never found out."

Lorena looked at her solemnly. "Perhaps you should tell me what you *do* know. I am sure it is all in your notebook, but it would be quicker for you to tell me."

Emily was always ready to share knowledge. "Well, we know Camazotz ordered one of his priests to make the amulet for him. But we think the priest was a secret follower of

Chac. He didn't dare refuse Camazotz, though. So he created the amulet, but he gave Camazotz only *one* piece and told him the other *three* were still being made. So, when Camazotz was banished, he had just the one piece—the crown. The two pieces that were found later and taken to Europe were shaped like a bat and an eye. And the fourth piece is shaped like a crescent moon. And, um, that's as far as we've gotten."

Lorena smiled warmly. "Yes, Emily. Everything you've said certainly accords with the legend. And it seems that the legend is actually true. I am very impressed with your translations. You have learned a great deal."

Emily flushed under Lorena's praise. "We had an amulet of our own, for a short while," she said, remembering another friend—Dominique—who had owned the little talisman. "It was a small stone plaque that had been found in Mexico and brought back to France. Vampires couldn't bear to be near it, but it had no effect on Camazotz himself. In fact, he destroyed it in the end."

"You had one of those?" Lorena sounded interested. "The records do mention them, but I have never seen one. They were a weapon of the priests of Chac, but in the long run it seems they did little good. Every time they were used to ward off a vampire, their power would drain a little. You would have found it could not be used for much longer. But the amulet of Camazotz—if it truly exists—is a very different matter."

"So, do you know what the four pieces do?" Emily asked eagerly. "You said you knew the legend."

"Each of the four has a meaning," Lorena told her. "The eye signifies that Camazotz is all-seeing. The bat depicts the form that Camazotz takes. The crown represents Camazotz's desire to rule the world. And the moon indicates that Camazotz is lord of the night."

Lorena's voice grew more solemn, and Emily held her breath. She felt as if a great secret was being revealed.

"An eye, a bat, a crown, and a moon, Emily. If the pieces are assembled in that order, Camazotz's mastery over creation will be assured. A darkness will fall over all the earth. The sun's light will no longer reach the ground. And that, of course, means that Camazotz and his servants will be free to roam at will." She smiled, but with no humor. "You see why Camazotz is so eager to complete the amulet?"

"Oh, yes," Emily breathed in horror. Her mind was full of the vision Lorena had conjured. A world where vampires could come and go at will. It was too terrible to contemplate. "How do you know all this?"

"It was carved around the cave where the Evil One lay," said Lorena. "I translated the carvings for Abran. But still, there is much in your parchments that was not there. Perhaps the missionary, Cabrillo, copied down the hieroglyphs from somewhere else."

"Did the cave carvings say where the four pieces were hidden?" Emily asked.

"No, they gave no clue," replied Lorena sadly. "I assume

the priests of Chac wanted to be sure that no one would ever find and assemble them." Suddenly Lorena was her bright and bubbly self once more. "And now, let us see if we can find out where the fourth piece is! These parchments may tell us, and if they do, perhaps we can make sure Camazotz never gets ahold of it."

"That's what I was *trying* to do," Emily wailed in frustration. "But the hieroglyphs suddenly changed. I was making excellent progress, until I couldn't understand the writing anymore."

"Show me where this happened," Lorena said thoughtfully.

Emily leafed through the parchments until she found the right one. "Here," she said, showing Lorena the place where the hieroglyphs changed. "Cabrillo has written a note in Spanish to say he copied these down from the north side of the Lunar Temple."

Lorena looked closely at the parchment. "That temple must still lie buried in the jungle. We certainly do not know where it is," she said. "But I think I can tell you why the writing changes. Cabrillo copied this section from a temple, so the information was written in the *priestly* form of the language. The rest of the writing, which you have been able to translate, was all in the *ordinary* form of the language, used by ordinary people. The priestly language was sacred; that's why it was different."

"So *how* is it different?" Emily asked eagerly. "It looks just the same."

"Exactly. The symbols *are* the same, but the constructions are completely different. Imagine that someone learned English and then came across another form where the words are all spelled backward, or written upside down. It would make no sense to them at all, but an experienced student could begin to decipher it, though it might take them some time." Lorena smiled roguishly. "And I am an experienced student. Look, I will show you how it is done. . . ."

They worked on the parchments for the rest of the day. By sunset they were close to the end. Lorena said that with just another day, they would probably finish them altogether.

"'The moon was hidden in the Lower Temple, in the place no follower of Camazotz would walk: the place of light,'" Emily read slowly, translating the priestly language as she traced Lorena's finger across the page.

Lorena smiled and nodded proudly. "Well done, Emily. You are learning fast. And this is the information we have been looking for. We must let Abran know at once."

"But do you know where the Lower Temple *is*?" Emily asked.

"The Lower Temple? Of course. The Temple of Chac is built on two levels, upper and lower. Everyone knows that." Lorena smiled mischievously. "Everyone except your European explorers, that is. We like to have *some* secrets."

Emily couldn't help laughing. "Is it far?"

"It will be no more than two days' journey," Lorena declared.

"I . . . I can't believe it's so simple," Emily said wonderingly. "And does everyone know where this 'place of light' is, too?"

"Why, yes," Lorena agreed brightly. "To someone who knows how the Mayan temples were constructed, it is obvious. The place of light will be at the top of a pyramid—the first place that the sun would hit. And that is why no servant of Camazotz would ever walk there. And now, we really *must* tell Abran!"

Ben held the bow in one outstretched hand. The arrow rested on his fingers. He drew the string back firmly with the fingers of his other hand and sighted along the shaft of the arrow to the wooden target.

"Only pull back as far as is comfortable," instructed Edwin. He stood behind Ben, bending down with his hands on his knees so that he could squint along the arrow, too. "Don't let your arm tremble or the arrow will go off course. And when you're ready, let go."

Ben let go. The arrow flew through the air with a *zip* and thudded into the target, almost at the dead center. He sent two more arrows after it and they landed only inches away from the first.

"Excellent, Ben. Well done," Edwin praised.

Ben didn't want to boast, so he didn't say anything, but it hadn't been hard. He had simply imagined that the target was Camazotz, and the arrows seemed to guide themselves.

Edwin turned to Jack. "Now let's see how you do."

Jack's first arrow went wide of the target. The next two flew far too long. He handed the bow back to Ben in embarrassment.

Roberto had been watching all this with interest.

"I think I might have just the thing for you, Jack," he said.

Jack let himself be drawn away, thinking that whatever Roberto had in mind, it had to be easier than archery.

Roberto tossed him a wooden stave, about five feet long. "Imagine this has blood rose on either end," he said. "You are marching through the jungle, when suddenly—"

Jack wasn't quite sure where it came from—Roberto moved too fast—but a leather ball flew at him. He instinctively swatted it away with the stick.

Roberto grinned. "A vampire flies at you from the dark!" he finished. "And I see you will need little training in this—"

Another ball, and again Jack sent it flying back. If those balls had really been bats, the vampires would have been killed.

Jack grinned. Perhaps it showed the difference between himself and Ben, he thought. Ben was thoughtful in a fight, rarely acting without a plan. His calm, calculating mind made him a good archer. But all his life, Jack had had to think quickly and trust his instincts. Roberto seemed to have realized that.

Roberto stood poised in front of him now, hands raised. "But the vampire might come at you in its human form," he said. "One bite—or one scratch from its claws—and you will be hurt, perhaps killed. You must strike it before it hits you—" And suddenly he was running at Jack. Jack dodged sideways and under. Roberto's swinging arm passed over him and Jack jabbed him in the side.

"You're dead, mate," he said with a grin. Sweat trickled down his forehead and he wiped it away with the back of his hand.

Roberto smiled grimly. "Yes, I am. But the vampires will come at you in swarms. Here comes another." He ran at Jack again, and this time he managed to jab him in the ribs before Jack could retaliate.

"You are already hot and tired," Roberto said. "The jungle will make you more so. But you must remember that the servants of Camazotz do not feel the heat. They do not sweat or hunger or thirst—save for your blood. They see in the dark and they will fight forever. You must never let your guard down, Jack."

They practiced for another hour. Jack had never learned to fight properly—running away had always seemed safer—

and though he was bone tired and sweating hard by the end of it, he also felt profoundly satisfied.

Ben wandered over to join him when Roberto finally called a halt.

"I think we're ready for them, Jack," he said with a grin.

A leather ball spun through the air one last time, heading for Jack over Ben's shoulder. Jack extended the wooden stave, stabbing the air just inches from Ben's face, which had acquired a startled expression. The ball was impaled on the end of Jack's weapon. He gave Ben his biggest smile. "Won't know what's hit 'em, mate."

CHAPTER FIVE

It was as Ben and Jack were making their way to find Emily that they heard the news: Camazotz might have three pieces of the powerful amulet, but thanks to the English guests, the Brotherhood would find and keep the fourth and final piece! Ben guessed that meant that Emily and Lorena had translated the parchment. Abran announced that they would march at first light the next day.

The Brotherhood's small army started preparing immediately. They knew where the Temple of Chac was, and it would mean traveling a jungle scattered with vampires.

Ben and Jack had helped make the weapons, then practiced with the weapons, and now they were pressed into service handing out the weapons.

"Off at dawn, eh?" Jack commented cheerfully as he set down a bundle of spears. "Sounds like an early night for us, then."

Ben agreed with a yawn. "I'm worn out. It's been a long day. Oh, hello," he added, glancing up to see his godfather approaching.

"Boys, could I have a word with you both?" Edwin

asked, and there was something about his voice that Ben didn't quite like. He looked quickly at Jack and saw that his friend had noticed it, too. But they stepped aside obediently to hear what Edwin had to say.

"I know this is going to disappoint you," Edwin said bluntly, "but I'm afraid you're not going."

Ben looked at him aghast. "But . . ." he began.

"Not going?" said Jack. And then they were both arguing at the same time.

Edwin held up his hands. *"That will do!"* He didn't raise his voice, but there was such power in his words it felt as though he had.

Ben quieted down, still fuming. But Jack refused to give up. Ben watched his friend arguing with Edwin and reflected that Jack had never let adults tell him what to do. Clearly he saw no reason to start now. Ben couldn't help but smile.

"You can't make us stay here," Jack was saying, "not after what we've done, not after everything—"

"Jack!"

And this time even Jack simmered down under the force of Edwin's glare.

"That's better," Edwin said calmly. "Now, I know what a blow this is to you, and you deserve an explanation. You have done great things in the fight against Camazotz. We wouldn't be arming for battle now if it wasn't for you two and Emily."

"Why all the training, then?" Jack demanded. "What we been preparing for?"

"You've been learning important skills for living in a jungle full of vampires," Edwin replied. "If you're attacked, you must be able to defend yourselves. But that's different from deliberately going into battle."

Ben broke in, his voice low and furious. "I made promises," he told Edwin. "Promises to myself. In Paris, I swore we'd find the fourth piece of the amulet first. And then Em and I promised Father that we'd avenge him—"

"And *I* promised your father that I would look after you two and protect you," Edwin pointed out. "I made that promise when you were babies, and it hasn't changed just because you've grown up. Now that Harry is dead, you are my responsibility, and that means I must keep you both out of danger. That responsibility outweighs everything else—even my obligations to the Brotherhood. I've talked to Abran and he understands that, for that reason, I'm not going, either."

"You ain't responsible for me," Jack said grumpily.

"I didn't make any promises to your family," Edwin agreed. "But as long as you keep company with Ben and Emily, then as far I'm concerned, you come under my protection as well. And that's all I'm going to say on the matter."

Emily found Jack sitting on a bench, playing idly with his evening meal. It was a thick, spicy soup, full of chunks of meat and peppers. Jack lifted up a spoonful and then tipped it slowly back into the wooden bowl.

Emily sat down next to him. "Uncle Edwin told me about your conversation," she said.

Jack looked at her gloomily. "Yeah," he muttered.

"How do you feel?" she asked.

"Better than him," Jack replied, indicating Ben with a nod.

Her brother sat a small distance away. He was moodily poking at the earth with a stick, his bowl of soup untouched on the ground beside him. He looked up when he heard them talking. "It's disappointing," Ben said softly.

Emily could tell *that* was a massive understatement. It was a bitter disappointment. The boys were trying to put a brave face on it, but they had been fighting Camazotz for so long, Emily knew how hard it was for them to be kept out of the battle now. "Camazotz will still need to be defeated," she pointed out. "Even if the Brotherhood finds the fourth piece of the amulet, he'll still exist. And Lorena and I are learning so much from the parchments, now that she's teaching me how to read the priestly language. We're bound to find more work to be done, more battles to fight. Really, all you're missing tomorrow is a boring trek through a hot and humid jungle. The Brotherhood's army will be there and back in a couple of days. You're better off here."

Ben sighed. "Em's right, Jack. It's not over yet. We can

stay, we can keep learning. *Lah yich saknik, maknik Chac*, and all that. And when it comes to it—well, we're part of an army now. That means we follow orders."

"Yeah, you're right," Jack agreed. "We got to follow orders." He picked up his spoon and started eating his soup. Ben did the same.

Emily heaved a sigh of relief to see that the boys had finally come to terms with the situation. "What was that rhyme you just recited, Ben?" she asked, changing the subject. "It sounded Mayan."

"It's a chant," Ben explained, repeating it so Emily could pick it up. "Apparently it clears the mind when Camazotz tries to take control of you. We could have used it in London—"

Suddenly Jack groaned. Emily looked at him, alarmed. "What is it?"

"Nothing . . ." He took another spoonful, then almost dropped it as he doubled over. "*Ah!* Ah, that hurt," he gasped.

Emily took his bowl away before he dropped it.

Jack sat up tentatively, grimaced, then clutched his stomach and doubled up again. "*Aagh!*"

"Jack! Jack, what is it?" Emily asked anxiously.

"Think I'm going to be sick . . ." he moaned.

"I'll go get someone." Ben was scrambling to his feet.

"No. No. I'll . . . be all right," Jack said, carefully standing up. "I think it were the peppers. They're a bit too strong for me. I'll . . . I'll go lie down."

"That's probably best," Emily agreed, still looking worried. "If you need anything . . ."

"I'll be right as rain in the morning," Jack reassured her, smiling bravely. "Good night, Emily, Ben." And he made his way slowly toward his tent.

The Brotherhood departed at sunrise the next morning. It wasn't like the military parades Emily had seen at home, with columns of men marching proudly off to war in neat red uniforms and shiny buttons. The soldiers of the Brotherhood knew the dangers they faced and the grim realities of waging war on a god who could command an army of vampires. And yet, the mood was positive. They had waited all their lives to fight Camazotz and now, finally, they could strike a real blow against him.

Suddenly the camp seemed empty. Only a small number had remained to guard the place—some of the older members; a handful of women, including Lorena; Roberto, who was in charge; and, of course, the three friends and Edwin.

"And now we must wait," said Lorena with a smile as Roberto shut the enclosure gate behind the departing army. She yawned. "It will not be an easy journey and I do not envy them, but I would love to be the first to see the fourth piece of the amulet."

Emily strolled slowly back through the deserted camp with her.

Lorena looked around. "Where is your friend Jack?" she asked. "I haven't seen him this morning."

"He took ill last night," Emily replied. "The food didn't agree with him. I'll go see how he is."

"That would be kind," Lorena agreed. "Take him some water, perhaps." She yawned again.

"Did you sleep badly?" Emily asked.

"I was up all night, going through the parchments again," Lorena explained. "I like to check everything at least twice. And now I think I will catch up on all the sleep I missed. Wake me up at lunchtime!"

They separated, and Emily headed for the tents that had been allocated to the three friends. Jack had been quiet that morning. She hoped he was just sleeping off the spicy food.

She crouched down and drew the tent flap back, peering into the gloom. "Jack? Are you awake?" she hissed.

There was no response. She could see the dark shape of his bedroll.

"Jack, are you all right?" she asked. "Look, if you don't say something, I'm going to get some blood rose and poke you with it."

Silence. Not even the sound of Jack's breathing. Emily made her way over to the bedroll and pulled the covers back. She stared down at the empty space where Jack should have been.

And then she spotted a scrap of paper lying on the pil-low. She snatched it up and turned it to the light. She recognized the scrawl. It was unmistakably Jack's writing. There was only one word, but that told her everything. The note simply said: *Sorry*.

CHAPTER SIX

"Oh, Jack, you *idiot*!" Emily exclaimed.

She stared at the piece of paper, then crumpled it up and flung it on the ground. She crawled out of the tent and stood up.

"Is Jack up?" Ben asked. He was walking toward Jack's tent, a bright smile on his face. He had had all night to get over his disappointment at not going to the temple, Emily realized, and now he was making a determined effort to be cheerful.

"Oh, er, he's . . ." Emily hesitated. If she told Ben where Jack had gone, Ben would be sure to set off after him. Then they would both be out alone in the jungle, at the mercy of jaguars, snakes, and spiders—not to mention vampires. And that would only make matters worse. "No, I think the stew was even stronger than he thought," she said. "He'll probably be in bed all day."

Ben made a face. "Rather you than me, Jack!" he called, leaning down to peer into the tent.

"Let him rest," Emily said, and she pulled the tent flap

down to hide the interior before Ben's eyes could adjust to the dim light.

"I was going to ask if he wanted to help make more weapons," Ben said as he and Emily walked away.

"Well, I think you're on your own," Emily told him. "Sorry."

"Oh, I've got Edwin and Roberto to keep me company," he said cheerfully. "How about you?"

Emily couldn't help smiling. "With a bit of luck, Lorena and I will finish translating those parchments today!" she said happily, and turned toward Lorena's tent.

She knew Lorena wanted to get some sleep, and sure enough, when she poked her head around the door of the hut, she could see Lorena sound asleep on the little platform at the end of the room. However, Emily saw no reason why she couldn't practice translating the priestly hieroglyphs until Lorena woke up.

She crept inside quietly so as not to wake her new friend. The parchments were on the desk, and Lorena's notes were in a neat pile next to them. Emily gathered them all up and left.

She found a shady place between the two huts and settled down to work. She was determined to get a grip on the priestly language that Lorena had begun to explain to her. She now understood that the words in the priestly language were made differently from those in the common language. The symbols were exactly the same, but the meanings were different. Words weren't spelled out letter by letter.

Instead, the different hieroglyphs represented concepts and ideas. For instance, Emily thought with a smile, in the priestly language you could put together the symbols for "brown hair," "Londoner," "obstinate," and "idiot," and you would have the word for Jack.

The problem was that you had to know—or guess—what the priest was thinking when he wrote down the words. It was like "the place of light" that she and Lorena had talked about. If you didn't know how a Mayan temple was typically laid out, it could be anywhere.

Ah! But this symbol here had to be Camazotz, she thought, feeling pleased with herself. The context was unmistakable. It mentioned He Who Walks By Darkness and his servants, the bats. That wasn't going to be Chac, the lightning bringer, or any other Mayan god. The passage that she was now working on was all about Camazotz. Unfortunately it didn't seem to mention any of his hidden weaknesses. It was simply a description of his priests and the ceremonies they conducted to worship him in his temple.

But . . . Emily's pencil hovered over a symbol next to the hieroglyph that meant "temple." It seemed to mean "lack of height" or "less high" . . . "*lower*," in fact. The passage was talking about Camazotz's *Lower* Temple.

"Oh, no," Emily gasped, as a horrific realization came over her. She frantically sorted through the other parchments, the ones that she and Lorena had translated the previous day. And there it was again—in the parchment that said where the moon section of the amulet had been hidden—exactly the same set of symbols. *The moon was hidden in the Lower Temple*, that was true, but it wasn't a part of Chac's temple at all. It was the Lower Temple of *Camazotz*.

Emily sat back, feeling sick to her stomach. The army of the Brotherhood of Chac was on its way to the wrong place.

Lorena held her head in her hands. Emily had taken her translation to Edwin. Desperate, he had hauled Lorena out of bed to double-check.

Lorena looked from the parchment to Emily's notes, then back again. "Oh, I am so ashamed! Such a silly mistake, but I have let you down so badly," she cried, almost in tears.

"Not just us," Edwin snapped, his despair giving way to frustration, "the entire Brotherhood. How could you—"

"Please, Uncle," Emily broke in quietly. She could guess how dreadful Lorena must feel and she didn't want Edwin to make it worse. "It was just a mistake."

He glared at her. "Emily, we cannot afford to make mistakes. We are locked in a terrible battle here with an inhuman enemy who can lose a thousand servants and still come back for more. If we lose, our men are dead—or *worse*!"

Emily looked pleadingly at Ben.

"Uncle Edwin, what's done is done," he pointed out. "The question is, how long do you think it will take for the army to realize the fourth piece isn't there?"

Roberto grunted. "Knowing Abran, it will be days and days. He is stubborn. He will take the Temple of Chac apart stone by stone if necessary."

"He might send for Lorena to come and help, once he realizes that the moon section is obviously not in the place of light," Edwin said. "But we won't hear from him for a couple of days at least."

"And we'll never catch up to them now," Ben added.

Edwin swore. "And Camazotz is getting closer every day! For all we know, he's back in the Yucatán already."

"We have no choice," said Roberto. "It is up to us to find the *right* temple and the last piece of the amulet." Then he grunted irritably. "But I must stay here. Abran left me in charge. I cannot leave."

Edwin looked at Ben. Ben stared back. Emily could see that they had both come to the same conclusion.

"I could go on my own," Edwin began.

Ben grinned. "I'd follow you, and how would you make me go back?" he asked.

Edwin sighed. "Very well. You, me, and I suppose Jack will want to come, too."

Jack! With everything that had happened, Emily had almost forgotten about Jack. And Ben and Edwin had no idea.

"Um, about Jack . . ." Emily began.

CHAPTER SEVEN

"I'm hot, I'm dripping, and my face is covered with bites and scratches. I'm fed up with every single leaf, twig, and insect in this wretched jungle. Oh, it's all right for you, yes, *you*, stupid bird with . . . with a stupid beak, and stupid . . ."

Jack pushed his way through the dark tropical forest, adding his own furious monologue to the general cacophony—the cries of birds, the hum of insects, and the crash of monkeys playing in the trees above.

A bird with a beak the size of its own body watched Jack pass by, then spread its wings and flapped away through the canopy.

Lying to Ben and Emily had put Jack in a very bad mood. He was used to having to lie to stay alive, but he couldn't remember ever lying to either of the Coles before. And pulling a simple little con, as he had by faking his upset stomach, was just too easy. He was quite annoyed with his friends for falling for it. It just made him feel even more guilty.

He had known he couldn't just show up when the army first set off. He would be sent back immediately. So, he had gotten up early and slipped out of the camp, carefully clutching his blood-rose spear and two water bottles. Not *too* early, of course, because it would still have been dark and he had more sense than to leave the security of the camp before the sun was up.

(*Not much more sense*, he thought bitterly as a branch snapped back and swiped him in the face, *but more than that*.)

Jack had sheltered behind a bush within easy sight of the enclosure. Then, when the army had marched past, he had crept after it. He planned to catch up with the men eventually, of course, but only after they were far enough away from the camp that Abran would have to let him stay.

Unfortunately the jungle was so full of twists and turns, and vines and creepers that threatened to catch his ankles and trip him, that Jack was finding himself falling farther behind. The members of the Brotherhood were used to making their way through the jungle. Jack was not.

Right now, for example, a great clump of bushes was blocking his way.

"I've had enough of this," Jack said out loud. "From now on, this jungle does what I says, and I says I'm going straight through." He put his hands out in front to protect his face and walked on. The branches scraped against his hands and legs, but he felt them gradually giving way. *Yes!* he thought. *Knew I could do this . . .*

He brushed aside a large leaf and abruptly came face-to-face with a spider the size of his hand. He stared, horrified, at its bright, fluorescent-yellow body and legs. Its knees were jet-black and shiny. Its teeth, Jack was sure, would rival a vampire's at a pinch. He could swear it was staring him in the eye, challenging him to go any farther.

He vaguely remembered somebody telling him that the rule of thumb in the jungle was that the more colorful an insect, the more deadly it was. This spider was *very* colorful.

"Beg your pardon, mate," Jack muttered. "Didn't mean to intrude." He backed slowly out of the thicket. He would have liked to turn around, but he didn't want to turn his back on the spider. So he kept walking until he was out and the thicket was well in front of him.

"Okay," he decided, "I'll go around, I think. Probably best."

He put his hand on a branch to steady himself and felt it slither beneath his fingers. *"Ye-ahh!"* he yelled as he jumped away. The branch was a python. It looked blankly at him from flat, reptilian eyes. Then it flicked its tongue and slithered slowly away into the undergrowth.

Jack could hear a strange, drumming sound. After a moment, he realized it was his pounding heart. He drew a couple of breaths to slow it down. In a jungle possibly swarming with vampires who had excellent hearing, there was no point in advertising the fact that he was full of warm, pumping blood.

"I *hate* this jungle!" he muttered as he carefully picked his way around the bushes.

A butterfly flew past. It was twice the size of any

butterfly he had ever seen in London. Its wings glittered with every color of the rainbow.

"Y'know," he said to the butterfly, conversationally, "I *could* just turn around and go back. What do you say?"

The insect fluttered around his head for a moment, then flew on in the same direction as the army.

"Yeah, you're probably right," Jack muttered. He held his spear at the ready and followed.

Jack had been careful to bring plenty of water with him, but he rationed himself to a few sips several times an hour. He would have loved to swig both bottles empty in one go, but he had no idea where his next drink would come from.

He was unbelievably thirsty. It seemed like all the fluid that should have been inside him was outside. Warm sweat trickled down his face, back, arms, and legs. His clothes were plastered to his skin. And none of the sweat would evaporate to cool him, because the hot, heavy air was already so laden with warm moisture.

The sun was high in the sky by now, beating down on the solid mass of leafy tree canopy below. The canopy was so thick that very little light reached the ground. But in spite of the perpetual shadow, the sun warmed the leaves, the leaves warmed the air around them, and the jungle grew steadily hotter and hotter. Jack remembered the Palm

House at London's Kew Gardens, where he, Ben, and Emily had gone to find the blood rose. Inside, it had been hot and humid, to mimic a tropical climate and allow its exotic plants to flourish. That had been like a cool spring day compared to the sticky furnace of the real jungle.

A humming shimmer of blue whizzed by Jack's face, making him recoil, until he realized it was just a pair of small birds. They were tiny and beautiful, reminding Jack of some wrought-crystal glasses he had once seen in a shop-window in London. The birds hovered in front of a plant with flowers like small bells and poked their long, thin beaks into the blossoms. Their wings beat the air faster than Jack could see, and the humming noise grew louder.

The birds flew off, and Jack peered cautiously into the plant. At the base of the flower was a pool of liquid that looked like water. He immediately felt twice as thirsty, but somehow he didn't dare try it himself. Apart from anything else, it had dead insects floating in it. "I know," he said to the plant. "Just call me Mr. Picky."

The day drew on and Jack knew he was falling danger-ously far behind. He picked up his pace as best he could and tried to ignore his grumbling stomach. He had brought water but no food, expecting to be with the army before long. It was well into the afternoon by now. At least the army would set up camp for the night, he thought. Then, finally, he would have a chance to catch up.

He froze as a distant scream echoed through the under-growth. It was not the usual cry of an animal. Jack recognized a human scream when he heard one. Within a moment it was joined by other agonized cries.

Jack clutched his spear in both hands and hurried forward, wondering what had befallen the army ahead of him. And then another sound drifted through the jungle—a sound that sent a chill to Jack's heart. It was the screech and hiss of a vampire.

He charged onward through the trees as fast as he could manage, but leaves slapped against his face, tree roots tripped him, and more than once his way was blocked by the undergrowth. Dimly, through the bushes ahead, he could hear orders being shouted, the sounds of battle, and the screams of the dying—human and vampire alike. Eventually the sounds grew louder and Jack realized he had nearly reached the battleground.

His sense of self-preservation kicked in then, and it finally dawned on him that there was no profit in rushing into the middle of the clash. He slowed down and crept forward carefully, until he found himself peering out through a bush onto the struggle between the Brotherhood of Chac and the vampires of Camazotz.

There were very few members of the Brotherhood of Chac left alive. The jungle heaved with vampires. In bat form, they swarmed around the army. There were at least four to every man the Brotherhood had. And though Jack wanted to run in and jab his spear into every vampire that moved, he immediately saw how futile that would be. One more human with one more weapon would make no difference. He would merely be bringing his own blood to the vampire feast he saw before him.

The vampires kept coming, flying down from the trees where they had clearly been waiting, protected from the sunlight by the dense, leafy branches. The Brotherhood's army knew how to fight. Jack could see that they had gathered in defensive formations, back to back, blood-rose spears and arrows toward the enemy. But the men were simply overwhelmed. No amount of discipline or training could bring success against such vast numbers of tireless enemies. Jack saw Abran, one of the last surviving soldiers, stagger as he drove his spear into two of the vampires. But even as they crumpled to ash, Abran went down beneath another six, and Jack felt sick to see them biting into his neck and sucking his blood greedily. It was not a fitting death, he thought, for such a brave and valiant leader.

And that was that. It was all over. Jack had arrived just in time to witness the end of the massacre. He turned away in horror, tears stinging his eyes, as the vampires gorged themselves on the blood of his dead friends.

Suddenly Jack saw a large bat swooping down toward him, its claws outstretched. He ducked quickly and the bat veered and turned for a second attack, screeching angrily. The creature hovered before him for a moment and their eyes met. Jack found himself looking into the red fires of Hell that shone behind the vampire's gaze. Then it hissed and swooped again, fangs bared and ready to rip Jack's flesh and spill his blood.

Jack brought his spear up quickly as it flew toward him, and the creature was impaled. For a moment, it just hung there. Then ash seemed to well up from inside it, and it crumbled away in a cloud of black, acrid power. Jack immediately crouched down, spear held at the ready, in case other vampires had heard. But it seemed his attacker had been alone, a straggler like him.

He glanced back at the lifeless bodies of the army. The vampires were still feeding, but Jack figured it would not be long before they started to scout around for survivors. The remaining members of the Brotherhood—back at the camp—had to be told the dreadful news. So Jack did the only useful thing he could. He slipped silently back the way he had come, until he was sure he was beyond the vampires' hearing, and then he started to run.

CHAPTER EIGHT

Everyone stared as Emily explained that Jack had gone after the army to help find the fourth piece of the amulet. When she finished, she braced herself for the storm she knew would come.

"Of all the irresponsible . . . stupid . . . hot-headed . . ." Edwin broke off in frustration, too angry for words.

Emily bravely turned to face Ben. Her brother was looking at her as if she had betrayed him. "Why didn't you *say*?" he demanded.

"Because you would have gone to bring him back," Emily told him simply.

Ben punched the air in annoyance, but she could see he understood.

Edwin sighed. "I apologize," he said to Roberto. "I was responsible for Jack. I should have kept a better eye on him. We both let you down."

"It's an imperfect world and we must live with it," said Roberto calmly. "Jack is off with the others and he will not be back for some time. You and Ben must try to find the Lower Temple of Camazotz and the moon section of the amulet. Emily and Lorena will stay here and continue with their translations."

Emily immediately opened her mouth to protest, but Edwin cut her off before she could say a word. "No!" he said flatly. "Listen to Roberto. It's bad enough that I'm forced to take your brother against my better judgment. I know you can fight, Emily, but without a doubt your greatest contribution is translating those documents. You never know what else might be in them. And as we have already learned, it pays to have two minds working on the translation, rather than just one."

Emily hesitated, feeling torn with indecision. She wanted to go with Ben and Edwin, but she knew Roberto was right about the translation.

"There is still the matter of where the temple is," Lorena pointed out tentatively, as if uncertain of how welcome her comments would be. "We all know the Temple of Chac. It is a large complex of buildings that we have known about for centuries. But the Lower Temple of Camazotz?" She looked at Roberto for confirmation.

"Such a temple has never been found," Roberto agreed. "Yet we know roughly where it must lie. This camp is built on the edge of Camazotz's kingdom. If you go southeast from here, you may find clues."

It wasn't much to go on, but it would have to do. Edwin was used to finding cities that had been swallowed by the jungle, Emily reminded herself. He was an eminent archaeologist—looking for lost buildings was what he did.

If anyone could track down an unknown temple in the middle of the rain forest, it was him.

"We'll get ready," said Edwin briskly. "Ben, we leave within the hour."

That night, Emily lay in her tent unable to sleep. It was as hot and stifling as ever, though the sun had long since set. But even if the air had been fresh and cool, she would have still been wide awake.

Ben and Edwin had set off in the early afternoon, as soon as they had gathered all the necessary supplies together. The two of them were disguised as ordinary Mexican peasants, riding a pair of mules loaded down with bags of food, water, and blood rose. Emily had waved bravely as Roberto closed the gate of the camp behind them. She knew the danger all too well, and Ben had gone off into the heart of it. It had weighed heavily on her all day.

Lorena had noticed her mind wandering and suggested that she leave the hieroglyphs for a while. "I do understand," she had said with a kind smile. "Come back when your mind is less distracted with worry."

But when Emily closed her eyes now, it wasn't Ben that filled her mind's eye. She saw brown hair and a roguish grin. It was Jack.

Emily smiled to herself as she remembered their first meeting. Ben and Jack had snuck into the house to talk to her. They had taken her by surprise and Jack had clapped his hand over her mouth to stop her from screaming. She had stepped on his foot to make him let go. Who would have thought then that he would become her dearest friend?

Emily sighed. That had been the first time the three of them were together. This was the first time the three of them had been apart since. Ben had had to go. Jack had not. "You are an idiot, Jack," she whispered into the dark. "Come back safely."

The night wore on, and Emily knew she wasn't going to sleep. She was too hot and had too many worries. She decided she needed a distraction and some human company.

Her mind made up, she crawled to the tent entrance and out into the night air. It was cooler outside, and she took a few grateful breaths. Then, because it was always unwise to linger in the open once the sun had set, she headed quickly over to Lorena's hut. She was pleased to see a light on inside.

The door of the hut was open and Emily saw that the light came from an oil lamp on the desk, next to the pile of parchments. But Lorena didn't seem to be around. Emily glanced over at the sleeping platform, but there was no sign of her friend. No doubt she was out stretching her legs or getting some fresh air herself. Emily sat down on the edge of the platform to wait for her return.

Something rustled under her fingers. She looked down in surprise to see another sheet of parchment poking out from beneath the covers of Lorena's bed.

"How did you get there?" she murmured, picking it up

curiously. It was one of the parchments she had brought from Paris. By now she would know the missionary Cabrillo's writing from across the room. But now that Emily came to think of it, she was sure she hadn't seen this particular sheet for some time.

She ran her eyes along the top line and immediately recognized the priestly language she had been working on so hard. That alone meant she should have seen the page within the last two days, but she didn't think she had. *Oh, well*, Emily thought, *perhaps it had been mislaid*. She would sort it out with Lorena when her friend returned. In the meantime, she idly began to translate the hieroglyphics.

She saw immediately that the page contained information about the amulet. That was useful, because knowing it helped her to interpret the more obscure symbols.

"'The pieces numbered four, for the four powers claimed by the Evil One,'" she read out slowly. "'The crown to symbolize his rule over the world of men . . .'" Emily found that this passage told her exactly what Lorena had said about the four sections of the amulet, but in more detail. If the four pieces—the eye, the bat, the crown, and the moon—were assembled in the right order, then "darkness would flow out upon all the earth."

But there was more. She concentrated on the next paragraph, frowning in concentration. "'Unknown to the Evil One, the amulet was wrought such that a different power might be summoned. A power that could destroy him forever,'" she read, then paused so that the significance of that could sink in. *A power that could destroy Camazotz!* she thought, hardly daring to believe it. It was just what they needed. She read on eagerly. "'The secret was carved on the rocks that surrounded his prison of a thousand years, but I write it down here so that Chac's priests may know the power of their god.'"

But before the vital information could be given, the hieroglyphics stopped. Emily looked around in frustration, rummaged through Lorena's bed for any more pages, then hurried over to the desk and looked through the familiar parchments there.

Unfortunately there were no more pages and no further hieroglyphs to tell *how* the amulet could be used to summon the power that could destroy Camazotz. The sheet she had just translated was the last of the parchments. Cabrillo must have been interrupted in his work and never got back to it.

Emily pounded the desk in frustration.

CHAPTER NINE

Emily hurried out of Lorena's hut, still clutching the sheet of parchment. At least her friend's absence was explained, she thought. Lorena must have been equally excited by this new information and come looking for Emily.

She stopped and peered into the darkness, slowly turning around. Lorena had to be somewhere around the camp.

A flash of movement caught Emily's eye. She stared and saw someone at the far side of the camp. It was definitely Lorena's familiar shape, round and bustling and heading toward the gate. Emily didn't want to call out and wake anyone, so she hurried after her friend.

The guards nodded to Lorena and opened the gate for her. Lorena walked through the opening and disappeared into the darkness beyond. The gate swung closed behind her. Emily was surprised. Clearly Lorena wasn't looking for her. And what on earth would she be doing outside the camp after dark? She must have read the parchment and worked out what it said. Could she be looking for Roberto, perhaps?

Emily approached the entrance. The guards knew her

by sight and opened the gate without being asked. She hurried forward and the gate was closed again behind her, leaving her alone in the darkness.

The lights of the enclosure were hidden by the thick hedge of blood rose. It occurred to Emily that being alone and undefended in the dark was a very bad idea. She quickly broke off a branch of blood rose from the bushes. Feeling better with a weapon in her hand, she looked around for Lorena.

The stars were out and moonlight cast a silvery sheen over the jungle. The area was littered with the stumps of trees cut down to clear the forest, and they threw pools of shadow onto the ground. Lorena was nowhere to be seen, but Emily had glimpsed her turning right out of the gate, so Emily turned right, too. She hurried around the edge of the camp, keeping close to the hedge.

And then suddenly she spotted Lorena. She was almost halfway around the edge of the clearing, as far from the gate as it was possible to get. She stood in the shadows beneath a tree so that Emily could only just make out her shape. Emily drew breath to call her friend's name just as a large bat flew across the clearing.

Immediately Emily ducked down behind one of the tree stumps. She wanted to shout a warning to Lorena, but she knew that to draw attention to herself would be a death sentence. So she watched, her heart in her mouth, hoping Lorena would see the danger and hide herself.

But Lorena had calmly stepped out from under the tree.

The bat hovered for a moment, blacker than the night. And then its form shifted and flowed, and suddenly a man stood before her.

Emily's grip tightened on the blood rose stem. She was ready in case she had to run to her friend's rescue. She waited for Lorena to turn and flee, but her friend approached the vampire eagerly.

"Were you successful, Javier?" Lorena asked quickly.

Emily barely recognized her voice. Usually so bright and friendly, it sounded suddenly cold and somehow greedy.

"Why must we meet two nights in a row, Lorena?" The vampire, Javier, responded. "You know you are meant to be careful. Why was your message so urgent?"

Two nights in a row? Lorena had met this creature the night before? Emily suddenly realized why Lorena had been so tired earlier.

"Were you successful?" Lorena demanded.

"The trap was a triumph," said Javier, sounding pleased. "The Brotherhood's army was exactly where you said it would be."

"And?" prompted Lorena.

"We exterminated them. Not a man survived," Javier told them. "We feasted well."

The words were like a sword in Emily's heart. *Jack!* she thought frantically. He had been with the army. Did this mean he was dead?

And another terrible thought was battering at her mind. Lorena had to be human—she walked around in sunlight—

and yet she was chatting calmly with a vampire! Emily tried to think of a reasonable explanation, or even an unreasonable one, that would vindicate Lorena. But there was only one explanation that satisfied, and it was terrible but true. Lorena was a traitor.

With that realization, Emily's heart hardened. The army, and possibly Jack, had been betrayed and murdered. Now she must learn all she could about Lorena's plans. And then she had to tell Roberto. She tried to concentrate on the conversation before her.

"But you did not request this meeting to ask about the army," the vampire was saying.

"No," Lorena agreed. "There may still be trouble. I told you the true location of the fourth piece of the amulet. Well, now the English girl has learned of it. Sherwood and the Cole boy are on their way to the master's temple now."

Emily stifled a gasp. Not only had the Brotherhood's army been sent to the wrong place, but the vampires were already searching in the right one.

Javier chuckled. "Just the two? We will find them before they reach the temple, never fear."

"Have you found the crescent moon yourself?" Lorena asked.

"No," Javier said with feeling. "We are searching high and low, but the clue was somewhat cryptic. There is no 'place of light' in the master's temple."

Emily slowly let out a sigh of relief. It was the one ray of light in all the terrible news she had heard so far. The vampires were looking, but they still hadn't found the final piece of Camazotz's amulet.

"And there is one more thing you must know," said Lorena. "The traitor priest who fashioned the amulet—he constructed a trap."

"*What?*" the vampire hissed furiously.

"Surely we knew he was a traitor—that is why he delayed its construction," Lorena said quickly.

The vampire glared at Lorena. "Just tell me what you know!"

"There is an alternative order in which the parts can be arranged. It will call down the power of Chac upon the master—"

"No power can challenge the master!" Javier declared, but now he sounded nervous.

Lorena snorted. "Say what you will. The amulet can be a threat to the master. I doubt he is aware of that."

"Almost certainly not. And he is close. We sense him, Lorena. We sense him every day, drawing closer to his land, to resume his rule. Do his enemies know of this?"

"No," Lorena replied decisively. "I only translated the parchment this afternoon, and I hid it from the girl. Besides, the parchment does not describe *how* the pieces should be rearranged for the amulet to be used in that way. That information is carved on the walls around the cave where the master slept. I believe there is little risk. The Master has three of the pieces already, and we will soon find the fourth. But still, he should be warned."

The vampire nodded thoughtfully, then smiled. "You have done well, Lorena. Our enemies are all but eliminated, and the hidden danger of the master's amulet is revealed— yes, you have done well. And we need your expertise at the temple. You may help us locate what is lost."

"Then may I have my reward? May I have my third bite?" Lorena asked, stepping forward eagerly. Emily heard her voice tremble. "You know I hate this earthly form. I long to be of the night like you and have your strength, your immortality, your *powers*. You have held the promise before me for so long. . . ."

"Yes," the vampire said softly. For a moment he sounded tender. "You may have your reward. You have endured the curse of the day and your weak, mortal body long enough. Tonight you will become one of us." He laid his hands on her shoulders.

Lorena tilted her head back, exposing her neck. "What will I feel?" she asked hurriedly.

"For a moment, just darkness. And then you will be—reborn!" The vampire opened his mouth impossibly wide and leaned forward.

Sickened by Lorena's treachery, Emily slipped away.

She would not cry, she told herself fiercely as she hurried back to the camp, her vision blurred by tears. She would *not* cry. There was no time for weakness. She had work to do. The men and women left in the camp had to be warned, because the vampires would come for them now that the Brotherhood's army was destroyed. And Ben and Edwin had to be found and warned. But first, she had to tell Roberto.

She hurried through the darkness, her mind racing, her thoughts on finding Roberto—and she forgot to be cautious. In her haste, she collided with a figure that had emerged from the trees.

"No!" she shouted, slashing with the stem of the blood rose she was still clutching, but it was difficult because the stranger was gripping her arms and holding them away.

And then a voice said, "Hey, Emily!" and Emily paused in doubt and wonder, for the voice was one she knew and loved and thought she would never hear again. The voice was Jack's.

CHAPTER TEN

"Jack! You're alive!" Emily dropped the blood rose and flung her arms around him. Then she pushed him away so she could look at him. His clothes were damp with sweat, his hair was matted, and his face was ashen, but he was *alive.* Then she remembered the danger. "We must get back inside the camp," she told him urgently. "Come on. . . ."

She hurried away, then realized he wasn't following. She turned back and saw that he seemed dazed. His head was slightly tilted, as if he was trying to make sense of something, and his eyes were not focused.

"Everyone's dead, Emily," he said. "They just kept coming, out of the trees, and I couldn't do a thing, not a thing. . . ."

"Jack, I know," she said firmly.

It seemed to get through. He blinked in surprise. "You know?" His voice was uncertain. "How do you—"

"Later!" Emily pulled him toward the camp. "Come with me. It's not safe out here." They reached the gate and hurried through quickly when it was opened by the guard.

"Where is Roberto?" Emily asked him urgently.

He looked at her blankly, and Emily remembered that not all the members of the Brotherhood spoke English. She tried again, *"Dónde está Roberto?"*

"Ah! En su choza," the guard replied. *In his hut.*

Emily and Jack hurried between the two central rows of huts, exchanging stories in rushed whispers. Emily was relieved to find that Jack seemed to be recovering from his ordeal. He told her he had made his way back to the camp through the darkness, guided only by his basic sense of direction. As he got closer, he had let his nose do the work. The smell of blood rose was unmistakable.

Emily told him about Lorena. And Jack didn't say anything. He just bit his lip and stared at the sky. His silence bothered Emily more than any amount of shouting and cursing would have done. She had never seen him look so angry.

And then a black shape swirled down out of the night. Emily ducked as her hair was stirred by the movement of the air. In a moment the vampire Javier stood before them, his eyes burning red and his fangs bared. Jack immediately stepped in front of Emily, his face set grimly, his spear held at the ready.

But the vampire made no effort to advance. "Young blood for your first feast," he said. "Enjoy them." His red eyes seemed to burn into Emily's skull and, briefly, she wondered who he was talking to.

The next moment, she had her answer.

"I will, Javier," said a voice behind them.

Jack and Emily spun around. Lorena was advancing on them, cutting off any retreat they might have had. The change in her was dramatic. She was the same size and shape, but her skin had grown pale and her once-friendly eyes now shone with an ominous fire.

"Come, Emily," she whispered persuasively. "Let me bring you the master's ultimate gift. . . ."

"How could you?" Emily gasped, her throat dry. "How could you betray us all to Camazotz?"

"How?" Lorena snapped. "You ask a Mayan *how*? My people were great under the master's rule, and what are we now? A race subject to foreign conquerors. But the master will make us great again. We will bring final darkness to this earth, the master will reign supreme, and his faithful followers will rule with him while you *cattle* cower in darkness for our sport."

Jack had heard enough. He pushed his way in front of Emily and raised his spear, pointing straight at Lorena's heart. "You want to get to Emily?" he said coldly to Lorena. "You got to get through me first."

"Ah, Jack, back so soon from your little adventure?" Lorena crowed.

"Finish him, Lorena," Javier said impatiently. "We are needed at the temple."

Jack jabbed at Lorena with his spear. She took a step back.

Jack grinned. "Ain't so great being a vampire, is it? When one scratch from a rose can do you in?"

"But there are two of us," Javier hissed behind him. "And only one of you is armed."

Jack turned quickly so that he could keep an eye on both vampires. He waved the spear menacingly from one to the other.

"Hang on, Jack," Emily called. "I'll be right back."

Jack glanced around quickly, just in time to see Emily dash into the alley between two huts. "Oh, thanks!" he shouted. He couldn't believe she'd abandoned him.

In the split second that Jack was looking away, Javier made his move. He grabbed the shaft of the spear and wrenched it from Jack's hands. Then he flung it away and turned to face Jack.

Hissing, the two vampires advanced together. Jack was caught between them, trapped by the huts on either side.

"I had hoped for Emily as my first," Lorena laughed, "but you will do."

Jack inched sideways toward one of the huts. He knew there was nobody in there to help — it was empty now, like most of them — but perhaps that didn't matter. Swiftly he turned and leapt up the single wooden step into the entrance. The thin wooden walls wouldn't normally offer much security, but Jack knew the ways of vampires. He was in a home. They were outside.

He turned back to the vampires and grinned at them through the doorway. "As I was saying," he told them, "it ain't so great being a vampire."

Javier put his head to one side and looked at the hut

thoughtfully. "Once, that would have been a tactical move," he agreed. "Sadly for you the owner of that hut died today along with his comrades. It is no one's home now." And the vampires started toward the doorway.

Jack swore and leapt for the hut's single window, which was in the wall opposite the door. It had no glass, just shutters, and they were open. He put his hand on the sill and vaulted through it. His boots thudded onto the ground outside.

There was a screech from inside, and a moment later two bats flew out the window after him. He was already running as fast as he could back around the hut, toward his spear.

Jack felt the claws of one of the vampires graze his shoulder, and he knew he was not going to reach the spear in time. But at that moment, Emily emerged from the alley between the huts, grasping a branch of blood rose. She swung it at the vampires over Jack's shoulder as hard as she could. The bats were forced to veer away sharply, giving Jack time to find his spear and turn back to face his enemy. As the bats swooped to attack again, Jack brought the spear up and around with impressive speed. One of the vampires managed to plunge beneath the spear's blood-rose tip, but the other was neatly impaled and immediately burst into a cloud of ash.

Jack grinned at Emily. "Thanks," he said.

"I just needed to grab a weapon," she replied. "One down! But we have to make it to Roberto!"

The second vampire hurtled out of the sky and transformed into Lorena just before it slammed into Emily, knocking her to the ground. In a flash, Lorena had turned to face Jack as he raised his spear to strike. She grasped the wooden shaft and pulled. It was so unexpected that Jack was jerked forward toward her, and Lorena's fangs sliced the air inches from his face.

"You will be mine," she hissed. "You will be mine."

She twisted the spear hard and wrenched it from Jack's grasp. Then she reversed the weapon so that the point was aimed at Jack's heart. She lunged forward, driving the spear at Jack, who threw himself backward out of the way in the nick of time. But he stumbled and fell.

Lorena laughed and tossed the spear aside. Her hands blurred and shifted into lethal claws as she stood, poised above Jack, while he lay helpless on the ground. In one swift motion, she was stooped over him, ready to bite. Jack saw Emily moving to attack her from behind, but he could tell that she was going to be too late. He tried to roll away, but Lorena's claws held him pinned to the ground.

And then Jack heard the whistle and thud of an arrow flying through the air and striking its target. Lorena suddenly arched backward, screaming, her face contorted with agony. Ash welled up through cracks that had appeared in her skin. And then she crumbled to dust. All that remained was the blood-rose arrow that had killed her. And the outline of Roberto, standing several yards away. He was lowering his bow.

CHAPTER ELEVEN

Ben felt tense. He was standing by his mule, deep in the humid heart of the jungle, and the surroundings were bringing back unpleasant memories of his first visit to Mexico. Here in the shadows, beneath the tree canopy, vampires were always a threat, even during the daylight hours. Ben held his blood-rose spear at the ready and stayed alert to every squawk, screech, or jungle sound that might warn of a vampire's approach.

Edwin had noticed Ben's unease and reminded him that when Camazotz or his vampires were around, the jungle usually fell eerily silent. Ben knew that his godfather was right, but still he couldn't relax. One brief moment of carelessness was all a vampire would need to destroy them both. So while Edwin pored over ancient ruins and crumbling buildings, Ben surveyed the shadows warily.

They were trying hard to look like two peasants, in straw sombreros and ponchos decorated with native designs. As Europeans, the two of them would immediately attract attention, and attention was the last thing they wanted.

Edwin ran his fingers carefully over the carvings on the stone pillar. Ben had been ready to ride straight past, but Edwin's instinct for finding ruins among the choking vines and creepers was infallible.

"Aha," Edwin murmured. "Yes, very interesting." He pushed back his poncho and dug a compass out of his pocket. He glanced at it, then back at the carvings, then up at the sun. Finally he looked back at Ben. "We're on the right track," he said. "Saddle up."

Ben climbed slowly back onto his mule.

Edwin swung himself easily into the saddle. "Giddyap," he said encouragingly, and the mule grudgingly shambled forward. Ben's followed without any instructions.

As they rode through the jungle, Ben settled into the rhythm of his mule's pacing. The movement was curiously soothing, and gradually Ben felt himself beginning to relax. He was still alert to the sounds of the jungle, but he began to enjoy the noise the monkeys made as they played in the trees and the raucous conversations of the parrots as they argued over tasty fruits or favorite perches. These natural sounds were completely different from the angry screeches of the vampires, Ben thought. There was no hate in the jungle creatures. They just busied themselves with the work of life rather than the business of death. *If a jaguar eats me, it will only be because it's hungry*, Ben thought. *And who can blame it?* he added as his stomach rumbled, reminding him that it was now some time since he last ate.

He realized that he had been so busy listening to the

jungle noises, he had lost track of their route through the forest. "Where are we going?" Ben asked.

"We're following the *sacbeob*," Edwin replied.

Ben remembered reading about the sacbeob before the first expedition. It was the network of Mayan roads that ran through the jungle. The Mayans had laid down routes of dry stone, starting with limestone rocks the size of boulders, then filling in the gaps with smaller and smaller rocks until there was nothing but pebbles underfoot. The sacbeob ran straight and true, elevated above swamplands and cutting through low hills. It was to the Yucatán what Roman roads had been to Britain—an engineering masterpiece that linked the cities together.

Ben looked down at the ground, trying to spot the road's surface. If this had ever been a man-made road, it wasn't obvious now. Like every work of humans in the Yucatán, it had been reclaimed by the jungle. But the undergrowth was only knee-high, not the usual choking cluster of plants and vines. And now that Ben came to look more closely, he could see that there was a kind of passage through the trees that allowed their two mules to walk side by side. "So where does this sacbeob go?" he asked.

"*Sacbe.* Sacbeob is the plural," Edwin corrected.

"So where does this sacbe go?" Ben tried again.

"I have no idea," Edwin said cheerfully. "But the Mayans wouldn't build a road that goes nowhere any more than we would. Sooner or later it will bring us to a city or a temple or to something where we can find clues. That pillar and the other ruins we've seen all suggest we're on the right track. We're venturing deeper into what was once the heart of Camazotz's kingdom."

They made good progress, stopping occasionally to stretch their legs or pick more clues out of jungle-smothered rubble. Looking at the fragments of ruins he could see, Ben was quite impressed by how grand the Mayan civilization had been and shocked by how far it had all fallen into decay. The Mayans had grown great with the power of Camazotz, but that same power had exhausted and blighted their nation. It was as if the entire land had risen up to reclaim itself once the people and the vampires were gone. The Yucatán itself seemed determined that the rest of the world should forget that the Mayans and their demon god were ever here.

Finally Edwin called a halt. The sun was setting; it was important that they make camp and arrange cover before it disappeared completely. Ben's nose told him there was blood rose nearby, and he soon found a full bush of the flowers. Then Edwin led the mules away to the other side of the track and tethered them to a tree. The mules were harder to hide than two humans. If the vampires found the animals, it was important that he and Ben were a safe distance away.

They didn't dare risk lighting a fire to cook food. Instead they ate salted beef jerky and biscuits they'd brought from the camp. It was washed down with tepid water that tasted of canvas and leather from their bottles. Eventually, as the sky turned dark, they crawled under the blood-rose bush, taking care to avoid the thorns.

"Lie on your front or your back," Edwin suggested. "It's the most comfortable way to spend a night on the ground." He settled on his front and soon fell asleep with his head resting on his folded arms.

Ben lay on his back, staring up at the thorny roof a few inches from his nose. Now that night had fallen, a whole new set of noises had started. Ben listened to them in fascination and decided that they were *almost* soothing.

There was a gap in the leaves above his face. By coincidence, it matched a gap in the leaf canopy, so he could see all the way to the sky. If he moved his head slightly, he could see the stars shining down.

A bat flew past his vision, and he froze. Then more flew by, and more still. They were vampires, no question about it. Ben recognized their size and their sense of purpose. But the shelter of blood rose seemed to be working, and Ben forced himself to relax.

The vampires were hunting, he realized, out on the prowl for the blood of some poor innocent. Someone somewhere in the jungle would not come home tonight.

Ben shuddered and tried to edge a little bit farther underneath the blood-rose bush. It took him a long time to fall asleep.

CHAPTER TWELVE

"So Lorena was a traitor!" Roberto sighed and shook his head sadly. The lamplight cast shadows across his face.

He had taken Jack and Emily straight back to his hut. The sounds of the scuffle between the vampires and the two children had woken him just in time for him to come to their rescue. Now they sat at his table and Emily explained the whole story, while Jack wolfed down a bowl of soup and some bread. He was famished and parched after his two-way trek through the jungle.

"And the army is gone. Betrayed and murdered," Roberto continued flatly, as if still trying to convince himself it was true.

"I suppose that means you're in charge of the Brotherhood now," Jack said bluntly. "What will you do?"

Roberto sighed again, then stood up and walked to the door. He gazed out into the darkness. "Yes, what will I do?" he said softly, more to himself than to Jack or Emily. He was not expecting an answer.

"You have to take us to Camazotz's cave as soon as possible," Emily said decisively.

Roberto glanced back at her dubiously.

Emily thought that perhaps he was unused to being told what to do by a girl, but she knew she had to convince him. "Lorena told the vampire that carved in the rock around the cave is the information we would need to use the amulet against Camazotz," Emily explained. "If Ben and Edwin are successful in finding the moon section, then it might prove useful for us to know how to do that."

"Why won't they just destroy the moon if they find it?" Jack asked.

Roberto snorted. He turned back to the darkness. "They might try," he said. "They will almost certainly fail. It was fashioned with arts that have long been forgotten. It is not a simple piece of jewelry that a man and a boy can break." He paused for a moment, then turned abruptly back to Emily. "I will take you to the cave," he agreed. "But now you must sleep. We will leave at dawn. Just the three of us."

"Ain't you going to raise the alarm?" Jack asked in surprise. "Tell the others what happened?"

"I do not wish to deceive my brothers," Roberto explained, "but for the moment, what good can the knowledge do them? We will let them live on in blissful ignorance for just a little while longer."

"But some of them might want to come to the cave, too," Emily suggested.

Roberto nodded wearily. "Precisely," he said. He frowned, and Emily saw how painful he found his next words. "After what has happened to Lorena, I am the only member of the Brotherhood that I know I can trust."

True to his word, Roberto led them off into the jungle as soon as the sun was up. The forest was already warm, but it was nothing like the dripping steam bath Emily knew it would become later. The night chorus of cries and calls had died down; the daytime chorus was just beginning. A red glow lit up the eastern sky and the leaf canopy was silhouetted against it, a strange black shape of seemingly infinite complexity.

They didn't talk much as they rode. Roberto kept his thoughts to himself. Emily could guess how sad and angry he must be feeling. And Jack seemed content to watch the jungle pass by from the back of his mule.

Emily's own thoughts turned to the amulet. If Ben and Edwin found the fourth piece, she thought, and if she and Jack and Roberto learned how to use the completed amulet against Camazotz, there was still the small matter of Camazotz having the other three pieces, and she couldn't see him politely handing them over. How could she and her friends get ahold of them? If they couldn't, and instead they just dropped the fourth piece into the deepest part of the ocean, would that be enough to stop Camazotz? Or would he eventually find a way to retrieve it?

A familiar, sickly scent drifted through the jungle, rousing

Emily from her reverie. She saw Jack perk up as he smelled it, too.

"Someone else has been decorating with blood rose," he said brightly.

"We are near the cave," Roberto told them.

Immediately Emily forgot her worries. She had heard so much about this place that she was extremely curious to see it. She remembered Ben's description. He had first seen it when out hunting with the archaeological expedition's guide, Miguel. The small deer they were stalking had disappeared into a thicket of what they now knew was blood rose. It had been planted all around the cave, completely obscuring the rock. It was like a nightmarish version of "Sleeping Beauty," Ben had said. To reach the cave, they had had to cut a path right through the barrier.

Suddenly the mules came out into a clearing, and Emily saw that the Brotherhood of Chac had been busy. A small cliff of limestone reared up out of the jungle floor. A semicircular area around it had been cleared, the trees and bushes carefully cut back. The cave and the stone around it were now clearly visible.

Emily marveled at the giant bat that had been carved into the rock. The creature's head was about five feet high, and its gaping mouth was the dark cave entrance itself. It was a natural opening—the carvings had been added around it later.

"Friendly," Jack commented.

Ben had reported that the cave mouth was surrounded

by the bat's head. He couldn't have known that the bat actually extended farther. With the blood rose cleared away, Emily could see the creature's wings outstretched on either side of its head. She was struck by how very lifelike that bat was. It had been carved in a style quite unlike any other Mayan carving she had seen.

Not all the blood rose had been cut back. The bat's wings disappeared into further thickets of the shrub. The space beneath the wings was covered with hieroglyphics that appeared to have been completely exposed. Emily assumed that that was why the Brotherhood had cleared no more of the blood rose away. They must have thought that they had uncovered all the writing. Now Emily hoped that there was more to be found, still hidden by the undergrowth.

"Where do you want to start, Emily?" Roberto asked. He seemed in no mood to waste time.

Emily scanned the rock. "Lorena didn't seem to know the amulet had another use," she said. "The information must still be hidden. We need to clear all the blood rose away from the stone."

Roberto nodded and tossed a machete to Jack. Emily picked up a knife from Roberto's mule, and the three of them went to work.

It was a difficult task. The blood-rose stems were thick and strong, and the roots ran deep, making it impossible to uproot the plants. However, it wasn't long before some hieroglyphs were uncovered. Emily immediately stopped cutting at the blood rose and started working on a translation. She worked more slowly than Roberto and Jack, so they soon pulled ahead.

It took nearly five hours, but eventually the cliff face was entirely uncovered. Emily was still hard at work with her notebook, about halfway through the newly revealed hieroglyphs. Roberto and Jack sat on a fallen tree and watched her, unable to do anything more useful. Roberto handed Jack a leather water bottle and he took a grateful swig. Then Jack stood up, stretched, and wandered aimlessly up and down the clearing—which took all of a couple of minutes. The cave was the only obvious item of interest, and he wasn't sure he wanted to get too close to it.

But then, why not? Camazotz was long gone, he reminded himself. He strolled over to the dark entrance and crouched down to peer inside. A rocky passage led into the cliff face for a few feet, then suddenly twisted away. He couldn't see any farther.

"Anyone been in here, Roberto?" he called.

Roberto looked up from where he was whittling on a stick. "Yes, a few people," he replied. "There is nothing there now."

"Mind if I have a look?" Jack asked.

Roberto shrugged. "By all means. I will get you a light." He took an oil lamp from the saddlebags, struck a light with his tinderbox, and lit the lamp.

Jack took the lamp from him a little nervously. Then holding the lamp in front of him, he bent down and shuffled into the passage.

The air on his face was damp and cool, which almost made him shiver. It was a nice change from the air outside, but he felt he didn't want to linger. The floor and walls of the cave were rough and he had to watch his footing.

Jack followed the passage as it curved to the right, then suddenly found himself in a much larger chamber. It was shaped like a wide, low dome. Here he could stand up fully, though the roof wasn't very far above his head.

Jack glanced up at the ceiling. It curved down on either side, meeting the floor perhaps twenty feet away in either direction. It was pockmarked with tiny holes. When Ben had been here, Jack thought, it had been thick with bats. He realized that the holes must have been made by the bats clinging onto the rocky roof with their hind feet for a thousand years.

He peered into the gloom at the end of the cavern but didn't particularly want to go in any farther to inspect. He could see boulders lying there with dark shadows behind them and decided he might investigate later if he got *really* bored waiting for Emily. Then he reentered the world of daylight, leaving the lamp just inside the entrance in case he returned later.

He emerged to see Roberto dragging a severed branch into the clearing. He was constructing a shelter for the night. Meanwhile Emily was crouched down on the ground several feet away from one of the bat's wings, examining the writing.

She looked up when she saw Jack and smiled. "Eye, moon, crown, bat!" she said happily. She tapped some of the carvings with her pencil. "Eye, moon, crown, bat. The eye that reveals all. The moon that shines light even in the darkness. The crown that will be stripped from Camazotz, and the bat that will be crushed by the power of Chac. I've found it, Jack! I've found it! Assemble the amulet in that order and it will destroy Camazotz!"

Jack peered at the carvings. They told him as much as they usually did, which was precisely nothing. "Well, that will be handy when we've pinched the other three pieces off him," he said. He squinted up at the tree line. The sun had just about set. Time for them to take cover. "I better help Roberto," he added.

He started walking toward the rough shelter, then stopped. Something was bothering him. The jungle seemed quieter than usual. And then he noticed a new noise—the rustle of dozens of leathery wings. "Roberto!" he yelled.

Roberto looked up just as a swarm of vampires erupted from the trees.

They were under attack.

CHAPTER THIRTEEN

"Into the cave!" Roberto shouted. He ran across the clearing to get his weapon from the mules. "Into the cave!"

Jack eyed the distance between the bats, Roberto, and the animals, and he saw that Roberto wasn't going to reach his weapon in time. Immediately Jack snatched up a branch of blood rose and ran forward to help.

But before he could reach Roberto, the swarm of bats had descended on the man, who cried out and fell to the ground. A second later Jack was among them, furiously swinging the blood rose at the vampires, driving the bats out of the air. He felt it connect with the creatures and heard their dying screams.

He was doing a good job of fending off the vampires, but Roberto was badly wounded, and Jack realized it would be impossible to hold back the vampires *and* help Roberto to the shelter of the cave. He was worrying about this when Emily suddenly came to the rescue with blood rose of her own.

"He told you to get into the cave!" Jack gasped.

"No, he told *us*," Emily corrected him, swinging her

branch through the air. "Let's go. You help Roberto. I'll keep the vampires away."

So while Emily wielded her blood-rose weapon, Jack stooped and managed to help Roberto to his feet. The man's face was drained and there was a massive gash across his shoulder. He staggered against Jack, who half dragged him toward the cave as Emily bravely held the vampires at bay.

Jack stumbled into the cave entrance. Once inside, he let go of Roberto and turned back to help Emily. While Roberto dragged himself farther inside, Emily and Jack stood guard. They followed him into the cave mouth, crawling in backward, always keeping the blood rose between themselves and the vampires. At the last moment, Jack grabbed one of the clumps of blood rose they had cut away and pulled it after him. It sealed the tunnel nicely. Finally they were safe.

For the time being.

Jack turned and crawled into the cavern. He saw the glow of the oil lamp he'd left behind earlier and picked it up thankfully.

Inside the cave he found Roberto lying facedown as Emily tended to his wounds. She ripped a strip of cloth from Roberto's shirt and tied it around his wounded shoulder. The cloth immediately darkened with his blood, but it seemed to stem the flow.

"Thank you," Roberto gasped. He pushed himself up and sat back against the cave wall. "I was too slow. I let you down. I am sorry."

"Don't blame yourself—" Jack began, but he was interrupted by another voice.

"Dear friends, do come out!" called a vampire down the tunnel. "We will not hurt you!" The tone was mocking—the vampire clearly wasn't even trying to sound sincere.

"Thanks," Jack shouted, "but we're all tucked in for the night. Maybe we'll come out tomorrow when the sun's nice and high."

"Why, what have we here?" called the vampire again. "A tinderbox! How useful!"

"My tinderbox," Roberto groaned. "I dropped it. They will use it to try to smoke us out."

Sure enough, a few moments later smoke began to creep into the cave. Jack peeked around the corner of the passage to see that the vampires had set fire to the blood rose he had dragged into the entrance, and they were now piling up more vegetation at the cave mouth and burning that, too.

Smoke stung Jack's eyes and grabbed at his throat. He coughed and drew back to join the others. They were scrambling deeper into the cave, away from the smoke. Jack followed. As he crawled across the floor, he felt smoke drift past his face. "There's a breeze," he said. "Does this place have a back door?"

"We never went in farther than this cavern," said Roberto. "It is possible."

Jack held the lamp up and shuffled to the back of the

cave. If there was a way out, then it could only be in one place—behind the jumble of boulders he had seen earlier.

He reached the rocks and held the lamp out to see what was behind them. As he leaned forward, the lamplight chased away the shadows, and Jack saw a narrow opening in the rock wall and a passage traveling at a steep angle down into the ground.

"Got something," he called, and waited while Emily and Roberto crawled up behind him. He peered into the little passage. It was too low to stand in, he thought. They would have to crawl. After about twenty feet, the tunnel angled away so that he could see no farther. And it was *very* narrow.

"There's a way," he told them. "But it's not very big. I'll have to crawl face-first."

"Oh, Jack!" Emily gasped. "Is there no other way?"

"Not unless you want to make friends with our chums outside," Jack replied. He squinted down the tunnel apprehensively. He had once made his way through the dark, vampire-infested sewers of Paris. Even they were preferable to this, he thought. At least then he had known that there was definitely a way out if he could only find it. In this place, he could only hope.

"Give me the lamp." Roberto was sounding weak but determined. "I should be the one to explore. There may be danger."

Jack looked at him in the lamplight. Roberto was bigger than him. If the little passage turned out to be a dead end and there was no way to turn around, it was quite possible that Roberto would never come back up again. And Roberto looked as if he could barely walk, let alone crawl down narrow rock tunnels.

"Nah, you two wait here," he said. "I'll be back as soon as I know what's down there. You can't be having all the fun." He winked at Emily and then, before Roberto could protest, he slid down into the tunnel.

CHAPTER FOURTEEN

Jack crawled and slithered down the tunnel, holding the lamp in front of him. Before he was halfway to the bend he had cracked his head on the ceiling twice and skinned the knuckles of one hand. He felt oppressed by the thought of so much rock above and all around him. It was like being buried alive, he thought. Then he desperately tried to concentrate on something else before panic overtook him.

The lantern struck an outcrop of rock and Jack froze. If it broke, he would be stranded deep underground, with no light at all. Luckily the flame flickered but remained alight. Jack resolved to take better care of the lamp in the future.

He reached the bend in the tunnel and peered cautiously around it. The narrow passage appeared to be a dead end. Jack groaned and rested his head on the floor. The faint smell of smoke reminded him that he, Emily, and Roberto couldn't stay back up in the main cave if they wanted to. They would soon be suffocated by the smoke or driven out to be slaughtered by the vampires. Neither option appealed, and as Jack reflected on this, he suddenly realized that the smoky breeze was quite strong down here.

He figured the air had to be coming from *somewhere*, so he scrambled onward to inspect the "dead end" more closely.

He reached the end of the tunnel and peered at the blockage in the lamplight. Then he ran his hands around it. He could feel a crack around the edges that made him reasonably sure it wasn't part of the tunnel. It seemed more like a rock that had fallen into the tunnel and now blocked it.

He carefully set the lamp down, then put both hands against the rock and pushed.

Nothing happened.

Jack gritted his teeth, braced his feet against the sides of the tunnel, and pushed again.

Had the stone moved? He was sure something had. He tried again, and this time the rock rolled forward and vanished. It fell with a loud crash, plunging away into a dark and empty space much larger than the tunnel. The rumbling echo of rock falling against rock reverberated around him. Then all was quiet again, and suddenly the tunnel had a mouth, and the lamplight showed only dark space ahead.

"Jack?" Emily's voice drifted down the passage. "Are you all right?"

"I'm fine," he called. "Wait a moment." He crawled forward and cautiously poked his head through the opening. He held the lamp out and looked around.

The tunnel came out in the wall of a cave much larger than the one Jack had come from. It was as if a long, thin, wedge-shaped chunk of rock had been torn from the earth.

The pointed end was below him and the flat end was the ceiling. The tunnel came out halfway down one of the sloping sides. Jack looked down and saw the rock he had rolled away. It was lying with a small pile of rubble in the point of the wedge a few feet below him. A stream of clear water was trickling past it.

He looked from side to side. To his right, he could see the end of the chamber. It was a blank limestone wall without another entrance or exit in sight. To his left, the wedge disappeared into darkness.

The breeze seemed to be blowing to the left, and the stream was running the same way. Jack hoped there might be another way out of the wedge-shaped cave beyond the area he could see.

"Come on down," he called back up to Emily and Roberto. "There's lots of room."

Even if there was no way out, he thought, they could stay down here for the night, out of reach of the smoke. He put the lamp down at the end of the tunnel to provide some light for his friends, then slithered down the slope into the stream below.

After some minutes he heard Emily approaching. He peered up the tunnel and saw her come around the bend on hands and knees, her head tucked down away from the ceiling. She was clutching several branches of blood rose in her hands. Jack reached out and helped her climb down into the cave. She looked around curiously.

There was a scraping and groaning, and then Roberto

crawled into view. It had clearly been a struggle for him to get down the tunnel.

"He's in a very bad way, Jack," Emily said quietly.

Jack just nodded. He could tell from the sound of the man's breathing that every movement was an effort. The vampires had hurt him more than he would admit.

"There, see?" he said with forced cheer as Roberto squirmed out into the open space. "Lots of room. We can just camp down here for the night and—"

"But I can still smell smoke," Emily said.

Jack sniffed and realized she was right.

"The cave above is almost full," Roberto gasped, trying to catch his breath after the exertion of crawling through the narrow tunnel.

The three of them lay propped against the sloping side of the cavern, legs braced against the other side of the wedge to keep their feet out of the water.

"The smoke couldn't fill up this cavern, though, could it?" Jack asked hopefully.

"We cannot be sure," Roberto replied. He sounded exhausted. Every sentence came out between pauses for breath. "The vampires can burn the whole jungle if they wish. And as soon as the blood rose is burned up, they can come down here whenever they like. It wouldn't take long for them to fly down here as bats."

"Great!" Jack sighed.

"How much farther do the caves go back?" Roberto asked.

"Dunno. I'm a stranger here myself," Jack said.

"They might go on for miles," Emily pointed out. "We could stay ahead of the vampires all the way—if they do try to follow us—until we find a way out. We just have to follow the draft."

She looked around, and Jack was amused to see her eyes shining. Only Emily could *enjoy* being driven underground by choking smoke and ravenous vampires. She was always thrilled by the opportunity for new exploration, he thought.

"We could be the first people ever to see this," she added.

"Yeah, the first people with the right kind of teeth," Jack put in. "Hey, why didn't Camazotz come down here? Why did he stay stuck up top for a thousand years?"

"It was not just the cave that held him," said Roberto, breathing more easily now. "Camazotz was held by the power of Chac. The ritual bound him. He could not move from the chamber until the thousand years of banishment had passed."

The light from the lamp flickered. They all looked at it nervously.

"How much oil was in there?" Emily asked.

"It was full. It has many more hours," Roberto told her.

"Hours, eh?" Jack said, trying to sound optimistic. If there were more narrow squeezes ahead like the tunnel they had just come through, Jack knew many hours could pass very quickly without them traveling far at all.

"We should keep moving," Roberto said, and hauled himself to his feet with a grunt. He almost collapsed, but Jack caught him. "Follow me."

"Yeah," Jack said through gritted teeth. He was supporting most of Roberto's weight, and the man was heavy. "Lead on."

The floor of the chamber flattened out farther on and the wedge was left behind them in the dark, though the stream still kept them company, trickling along down one side of the cavern. Soon the ground was covered with a host of sharp, pointed rocks almost as tall as Roberto. Emily said they were called stalagmites. More pointed rocks—stalactites, apparently—hung from the ceiling above. They looked razor sharp and reminded Jack uncomfortably of teeth.

The chamber narrowed to become a tunnel—though a wider, higher one than the narrow passage of earlier. Then there was a hole in the rock even smaller than the one they had come through. The stream ran merrily into it and the friends followed. They splashed along the tunnel until it emerged about five feet above the floor of a larger cavern. The stream splashed down into a small pool before flowing away into the darkness. The friends clambered down into the pool, where Jack was fascinated to glimpse strange, almost transparent fish.

This new cave was so large that the lamplight didn't reach the sides or the ceiling. They followed the stream across the cave floor. Jack noticed that the rock around them had been twisted and rounded by the water's passage. Clearly the little stream had once been a river.

Strange shapes loomed out of the darkness, like limestone sculptures of giant toadstools, and still there was no sign of any opening to the outside world.

The friends crawled on through low tunnels, scrambled over rockfalls, and wandered through lofty caverns like vast underground cathedrals. Jack lost track of time, but he noticed that Roberto's strength was failing. Even with Jack and Emily's support, the young man was moving more and more slowly. And Jack could see that Emily was tiring, too. He prayed they would find a way out of the caves soon.

Eventually they reached a long, narrow chamber where the stream had carved out a small channel for itself, but then they came to a waterfall. The stream plunged over the side of a smooth, rounded boulder twenty feet wide. The sides of the chamber narrowed to this point so that there was no way around it. The surface of the boulder was slick with water, and the only way down was to slide. They could just see the bottom and there was nothing like a handhold in between.

"Got to be another way," Jack said, looking from side to side. "Got to be . . ."

But there wasn't, and it was quite clear that this was the only way forward.

"We'll have to slide down," Emily said practically. "There's no other way."

"Yeah," Jack agreed unhappily. He looked at the lamp he was still holding. If he slid down the waterfall, he would hit the bottom hard. If he was holding the lamp, the best he could do was to use one hand to protect it from the impact. "Well, let's do it," he said. "I'll go first."

He and Emily helped Roberto sit at the top of the smooth slope. The two of them sat down beside him, and then Jack pushed himself off.

Jack felt himself sliding, then falling, then sliding again, and his feet slammed into the rocky floor at the bottom. He pitched forward and rolled over, still trying to hold the lamp out of the way. The metal base of the lamp clanged against the ground. Jack watched anxiously as the light inside guttered, but then the flame took hold again and threw out its usual steady glow.

He breathed again. "Come on down," he called, "the water's lovely!"

Emily threw the blood rose down after him, and a couple of seconds later she had joined him herself. She had both hands to spare for the job and she came down more gracefully. "I'm very worried about Roberto," she whispered. "I couldn't say this before without him hearing, but I think his strength is fading."

Roberto came slithering down behind her. He fell limply, with his body twisted, and he slammed into the ground sideways with a cry of pain. Then he lay still.

Emily and Jack hurried to help him up and out of the water. He slumped to the floor between the two boulders.

"You have to go on by yourselves," he croaked. "You cannot take me."

"No! No, Roberto, we'll all keep going together," said Emily.

"We're not going to leave you," Jack declared at the same time.

Roberto's head lolled. "I just need to rest," he whispered. "Then I will be strong again. But you two cannot afford to wait. You must find the way out. Then, perhaps, you can get help for me. But if the vampires come . . . they must not find . . . you. . . ." His breath died away in a sigh and his head fell back.

Jack put his head to Roberto's chest and listened. He could hear a faint heartbeat. "He's alive," he said with relief.

"But we'll never get him out now," Emily said.

"No," Jack agreed. "He were right, Emily. We've got to leave him."

Emily stared at him. "Leave him in this place? We can't!"

Jack shared her feelings completely, but he really didn't see how they had a choice. "Look," he said, "if we can escape, find a way out, then we can come back for Roberto. But if we all stay here, then we could all die. And Roberto can't go any farther."

Emily looked as though she was going to argue, but after a moment she bit her lip and nodded. She looked sadly down at the unconscious man, then crouched and put a stem of blood rose into his hand. "Come on," she said, and walked off into the darkness.

Jack hurried after her with the lamp.

The cave narrowed again to a thin crack, tall but not wide. They had to slide along it, with the rock only inches from their faces. Eventually the crack hit a stone wall and the stream vanished into a tiny hole at its base. There was a larger opening directly above them, like a chimney of rock. Jack handed the lamp to Emily and scrabbled his way up, bracing his hands and legs against the sides of the chute. It was only a few feet, and then he found himself in a wider chamber again. Emily passed the lamp up and he set it down on a small ledge. Then he reached down and helped her climb up after him.

Once Emily was safely up, Jack held the lamp high and let the light illuminate the new cave. It was domed, with a high, curved ceiling and a flat floor dotted with stalagmites. A dark pool of water filled one corner. There was no obvious exit.

"Which way now?" Emily asked.

"Let's see," Jack replied. They walked slowly around the cave, looking for an exit. There was still a faint draft but it was impossible to tell the direction. It seemed to circulate in the cave.

"There must be a way out," Emily said unhappily. "We can't have come all this way for nothing."

"Yeah, I know," said Jack. "We just have to—" And then his foot slipped on a slick patch of wet stone and he slid over backward. His yell echoed around the cave as the lamp flew from his grasp and smashed into the stone floor. The little pool of spilled oil flared for a moment, then it was gone.

"*No!*" Jack roared. "Stupid, stupid, *stupid!*" His voice echoed around the cavern, but the light was gone for good.

"Don't blame yourself, Jack."

He heard Emily trying to be brave as he sat up. It was *very* dark. The blackness around them seemed absolute, like a smothering blanket. "Where are you?" he asked, looking blindly around him.

"Over here," Emily replied.

They crawled toward each other, following the sound of the other's voice. Their fingers met and they huddled together on the stone floor.

"I dropped the blood rose," Emily whispered. "I don't know where it is."

"Least of our worries," Jack muttered.

"We've still got the draft," Emily pointed out. "We can still try to follow it."

"Yeah. Maybe we can find it better in the dark," Jack said hopefully. "You know, like blind people can hear better. . . . What's that?"

There was nothing there when he looked at it directly.

But out of the corner of his eye Jack could definitely see a very faint patch of light. He pointed it out to Emily.

"Oh, yes, I can see it, too!" she exclaimed in excitement.

They shuffled across the stone floor toward it until Jack's probing fingers suddenly disappeared into chill water. They were at the edge of the pool he had seen earlier.

"There *is* a light!" Emily said.

"Yeah . . ." Jack replied uncertainly. He crouched down and squinted. He had to put his head against the surface of the pool, and water lapped against the side of his face, but now he could see that the water flowed under the rock wall of the cavern and then out into somewhere silvery. "I think it's moonlight," he said. "I think it's open air out there."

"Then let's swim," Emily said brightly.

Jack heard the splash of a body entering the water. "Emily?" he called in surprise.

"I'm here." Her voice was right by his feet. "It's not deep. Just jump in."

Jack had no intention of just jumping in. He lowered himself in very slowly. The water felt like a sheath of ice sliding up his body. He gritted his teeth as it reached his waist, his chest, his shoulders. And then his feet touched the bottom.

"Come on," said Emily. She took his hand under the water and led him toward the sliver of moonlight. As they drew closer, he was just able to make out her silhouette.

Emily crouched down so that her eyes were level with the surface of the water as she peered under the cave wall.

"We'll have to hold our breath for this next part," she said. "Are you ready?"

"As I'll ever be," Jack responded grimly.

"Then one, two . . ." Emily took a deep breath and plunged beneath the water, pulling Jack after her.

The cold water slid up his face and over his head. He hated being submerged in the dark, but suddenly they were out on the other side and Jack found he could stand up straight. Best of all, above him, far away, he could see the stars. "We're out!" he shouted joyfully. His voice bounced back from the rocks around them. "We're free!"

Their eyes adjusted quickly to the moonlight. Soon they could see the rocks dark against the silver surface of the water. They waded toward them and pulled themselves out. They could already feel the warmth of the jungle air against their skin, though they shivered in their damp clothes.

"How long were we down there, do you think?" Emily asked.

"Hours and hours," Jack replied. "I thought it would be light by now. Unless . . ."

"Unless what?" she pressed.

"Unless we was down there for the whole night and the day. We must have been. And now it's night again."

Emily was peering up at the sky. "I think we're at the bottom of a cenote," she remarked.

"Think we'll be able to get out?" Jack asked, remembering how steep and sheer the sides of a *cenote* could be. It would be a horrible irony to escape the caves only to die of starvation at the bottom of a pit.

"Let's rest and wait for the daylight," Emily suggested. "Then we can explore."

"You want light?" demanded a harsh voice in the darkness.

Jack heard Emily gasp as he bit back his own cry of surprise. He strained his eyes, peering into the dark in an effort to see who had spoken.

And then a torch flared and burned with an orange flame. Its flickering light chased away the blackness, revealing the dark figure that held it—and many, many more.

As Jack looked up and around, he saw that he and Emily were in some kind of amphitheater. It was full of people standing silently, staring at them. Bats wheeled overhead, then shifted and transformed into men.

"Jack . . ." Emily whispered in horror.

Jack gazed up at the silent audience and saw with a chill that the torchlight shone red in a hundred vampire eyes.

CHAPTER FIFTEEN

The trees stopped so suddenly that Ben and Edwin were caught by surprise. They looked beyond the trees at a small village in a large clearing.

They had been traveling along the sacbe all day. Sometimes Ben would catch a glimpse of the antique stone-work beneath the undergrowth and the mules' hooves, sometimes not. The day was winding down. Soon it would be the end of their second full day on the trail and their third night of sleeping under bushes.

Or perhaps they could stay in this village, Ben thought. Everyone knew a private home, even if it was just a hut, was the safest defense against the vampires.

The place was little more than a collection of huts around a central marketplace. The stones of the sacbe had been torn up to make a waist-high wall around the clearing. The jungle growth came right up to it. Ben and Edwin were standing in a gap in the wall, the gateway into the village. Most of the huts stood on little platforms with crawl spaces beneath, like the huts in the Brotherhood's camp. It was a simple defense against snakes and other crawling creatures.

The buildings seemed to be thrown together out of adobe covered with white plaster. The roofs were thatched. There was one slightly larger, more European-looking building that was clearly the local church. It was square with a pointed, tiled roof and a cross hanging over the door.

The place was obviously not ancient Mayan. The fact that the locals had casually torn up the old road showed that. But it also looked more settled than the Brotherhood's camp, as if it had been around longer. In fact, Ben thought, it looked like a typical village.

Edwin slipped off his mule and walked it behind the wall. Ben's mule, which was accustomed to following the one in front, ambled after it. Ben dismounted and crouched beside Edwin behind the stones, peering out.

"If anyone saw us . . ." Edwin muttered.

"It might just be an ordinary village," Ben pointed out. But he understood why Edwin was cautious. They were in the vampire heartland, after all. "Look," he said. He nudged Edwin and pointed. Over to one side, in the shadow of some trees by the edge of the clearing, was a cattle pen. Scrawny cows ambled about in it, munching on hay or just staring into the distance.

"Vampires wouldn't keep cows, would they?" Ben asked.

"They might," Edwin told him. "Vampires don't just drink *human* blood. Sometimes they can't get humans and then they'll take any blood at all."

"Oh," Ben said, kicking himself. Of course. Humans kept cows for milk; vampires kept them for another kind of drink. There was nothing to indicate which kind of cows these were.

"And it's strange," Edwin commented. "Where do you think all the people are?"

"Perhaps they have fields in another clearing?" Ben suggested hopefully. "They could be working there."

"Everyone?" Edwin asked skeptically. "The women? The children? It's not very likely." He drummed his fingers absently on the stone. "We can't go around easily; the trees are too thick. But I don't really want to take you through."

"Why not?" Ben asked.

Edwin sighed and lifted Ben's sombrero. "Fairest hair I ever saw on a Mexican," he remarked, and put the hat down again. "And even with the sombrero on, your skin is too light and your Spanish accent wouldn't fool anyone."

"I can keep quiet," Ben suggested.

Edwin smiled. "I know you can. And there's nothing else to do. We'll just ride on through, and if anyone speaks to us, let me do the talking. Come on."

They pulled their hats down low over their faces, climbed back onto the mules, and rode forward. Because the stones had been lifted up, the ancient sacbe just seemed to evaporate in front of them. They were riding along a muddy track across a clearing of beaten earth.

Some of the buildings around the edge of the village, close to the wall, were obviously in disrepair. The roofs had collapsed, or holes had appeared in the walls where the mud bricks had crumbled. The huts near the middle of the village were in a better state. Someone was still looking after them. But Ben realized what was *really* wrong with the place as they drew close to its center. It wasn't the lack of people. It was the silence. There were the cattle, penned over to one side, and every now and then one of the cows would make a low, mournful noise. But there was nothing else — no chickens squawking, no pigs snuffling their noses in the dirt, no birds singing.

The track turned into the village's main street. They passed buildings on either side. The doors were shut tight and the windows were blank and black. It was like being stared at by unseeing eyes. And still the only noise was the mules' hooves scuffing the dirt and the occasional animal grunt from the cattle pen.

Ben couldn't see the sun without looking up, and he didn't want to do that. But the shadows on the ground were long and there was a red tint in the air that told him sunset was near. If the village really was deserted, he thought, perhaps they could hide in one of the huts for the night. If they claimed it as their own, would that make it a private home and protect them from vampires?

They emerged into the village square and immediately realized there was no possibility of staying the night here. In the center was a plinth that had probably once held a statue—a local village hero, perhaps, or a cross or memorial. Whatever had once stood there, it was now gone, and in its place was a large statue of a bat.

"Keep going," Edwin muttered. "Just *keep going*." It was good advice, because against all sense, Ben wanted to rein in his mule and stare.

They continued on around the side of the square, and Ben allowed himself a quick, sideways glance at the statue. It reminded him of the bat section of Camazotz's amulet, though the craftsmanship was lacking. The amulet was solid gold, but this statue was crudely modeled clay and wood. It had hind legs very like a man's, and it stood on its two feet with its body upright and its wings spread out. There was no question of who it was meant to be.

"They worship Camazotz," Ben murmured.

"So they're probably vampires," Edwin agreed. "Keep riding. We're safe enough in the sunlight."

They left the square and passed between the huts on the other side. And then when they were leaving the village and crossing the far side of the clearing, Ben realized he had scarcely been breathing, though his heart was pounding so loudly he was sure Edwin could hear it. But now all they had to do was keep going, follow the track. . . .

But the track had disappeared.

Edwin noticed at the same time. "Unbelievable!" he muttered, glancing at the ground. "Never mind, Ben. Whatever you do, just keep going."

The track had dwindled away as they entered the village,

and they had both presumed it simply carried on through. It would emerge again on the other side and they could continue on into the jungle. But ahead of them now was a blank wall with no obvious way through. The track must have swung to the left or the right at some point. It probably led out of the square in a different direction from the one they had taken. Wherever it was, it certainly wasn't beneath their feet at that moment.

Ben glanced quickly at the sky. The sun was very low.

"We have to get out of this clearing, Ben," Edwin said urgently. "Look around. See if you can find the opening in the wall."

Ben peered around the edge of the clearing to their left, while Edwin looked to the right.

"I think I see it," Ben whispered after a moment, nudging Edwin. He pointed over to the side of the clearing, about halfway between where they had entered and where they were now. It was like the gate they had come through, wide enough for a pair of mules. At the creatures' usual pace it would take about five minutes to get there.

Edwin glanced up at the sky, then back at the gap. He was clearly assessing whether they could reach the gap before the sun set and the vampires awoke. But the red sun was right on the tree line. "No time," he cursed. "No time." He looked back the way they had come.

"Come on," he said unexpectedly. "Quick." He leapt off his mule and seized its halter, dragging the creature behind him. The surprised animal moved after him at a slightly faster pace than its usual amble. Ben and his mule followed.

Edwin was heading for one of the ruined buildings. It was larger than most—perhaps it had been a storeroom or a small barn when the village was still inhabited by humans. It was built on the ground, not elevated on stilts, and Ben realized what Edwin's plan must be. The roof of the building was largely intact, but some of the walls had fallen in. The wall that faced the village, however, was still standing. There would be room for Edwin, Ben, and the mules to squeeze inside without being visible from the village. What was left of the roof would shelter them from the gaze of spying bats.

Ben did not want to spend the night a matter of yards from a village full of vampires, but he knew they had no choice.

"Sorry," Edwin whispered as they led the mules into the building. "My fault. Got careless."

Ben just shrugged. He pressed his face to a crack in the mud wall that overlooked the village. Edwin carefully tethered the mules, then came to join him.

Now that the sun had set, the place was coming to life. Vampires emerged from the shadows and dozens of pairs of red eyes shone in the gloom. From their clothes, Ben thought, they looked like typical Yucatán peasants. Unfortunately they had left that way of life behind some time ago.

They gathered in the village square as if they were in a

makeshift procession. One or two broke away and headed for the cattle pen.

"No!" cried a harsh voice. Ben saw a separate group of seven men move forward into the twilight. They were dressed differently from the others. Their leader wore an elaborate headdress and a long, sweeping cloak. In one hand he carried a staff with a carved bat's head at the tip. The men behind him were dressed similarly. It was all very grand and ceremonial. Ben guessed that the leader must be some kind of priest. He was in human form, but his face displayed the features of a vampire bat. It was he who had spoken.

Ben strained his ears to hear the response, and even his rusty Spanish was good enough for him to understand.

"We hunger! We have not eaten all day," pleaded one of the rebuked men.

"The purification requires hunger," snapped the priest. "The temple must be cleansed for the master's return. Come."

The hungry men reluctantly returned to the procession, and the villagers slowly trooped out of the clearing.

Ben and Edwin stared at each other in the gloom.

"A whole village of vampires!" Ben exclaimed softly.

"You sound surprised," Edwin muttered drily.

"Well . . ." Ben frowned. He had known vampires to live in caves and sewers — even in grand houses in London. But a Mexican village seemed so *normal*.

"I doubt it's been a village of vampires for long," Edwin said, as if reading Ben's mind. "I'll wager that until a couple of months ago, this place was a perfectly normal, happy little town. And then the vampires came and changed it. Did you notice they were all adults? No children?"

It hadn't occurred to Ben, but now that Edwin mentioned it, it did seem odd.

"Vampires don't grow and they don't have babies," said Edwin. His voice was hollow and dark. "The young people here would have been slaughtered for food."

While Ben was contemplating the terrible truth, Edwin moved to the door of the barn. "Come on," he said.

Ben stared at him. "Are we leaving?" he asked hopefully.

Edwin smiled, his teeth a flash of white in the darkness. "Yes," he replied.

Ben sighed with relief and started to climb to his feet.

Edwin was unbuckling a pack from the saddle of one of the mules. He threw it to Ben. "Dried meat, some water. You never know how long we'll be," he said, and turned back to get another pack for himself.

"Where are we going?" Ben asked suspiciously.

"You heard the high priest," Edwin told him. "The temple is nearby and they're going to purify it. If we follow them, they'll lead us right to it."

The vampires proceded out of the village and into the jungle. They disappeared into the undergrowth through the hole in the wall that Ben had spotted earlier. He and Edwin waited for a few moments, then drew out their blood-rose spears and followed cautiously.

Going back into the jungle was like disappearing down a hot, dark tunnel. Edwin and Ben made their way through the undergrowth as quietly as they possibly could. After a few minutes, Edwin stopped abruptly.

Ben bumped into his godfather and peered around him to see why he'd halted.

Edwin turned and put his mouth to Ben's ear. "I think there's a light up ahead," he whispered. "Come on."

Ben nodded, though Edwin could not have seen him in the darkness, and they slowly felt their way forward.

There *was* a light in the distance—before long, Ben could see it himself. It was a yellow glow rising up from the ground.

Soon the trees parted, and Ben found himself out in the open. He could see the stars, and a fresh light breeze ruffled his hair. And now he could see why the light seemed to come from the ground.

A wide pit lay before them. Its limestone walls flickered with torchlight shining up from the depths. They were on the lip of a cenote. Edwin led Ben around the edge, always careful to keep far enough back so that they wouldn't be seen by whoever or *whatever* was down below. Once they were a safe distance away from the path they had taken, Edwin lay down on his stomach and crawled forward. Ben followed his example, and together they peered very carefully over the edge of the water hole.

The sides of the cenote were sheer, and near the top were the usual rough stones of the Yucatán. Below that, however, the walls were carved. They were covered with hieroglyphs and pictures of Camazotz in many guises — man, bat, and something monstrous that combined the features of both. Ben wondered if this was the demon god's true form. At the bottom of the cenote there was a natural platform of stone next to a pool of dark water. A large, square slab of rock, like an altar, stood on the platform, and it was surrounded by vampires. Flames flickered in a burning brazier next to the altar stone.

"This is it," he whispered. "We've found the temple of Camazotz!"

Edwin nodded and signaled for Ben to be silent. The cenote amplified even the smallest sounds.

Ben looked quickly around the sides of the pit for a way down, but he couldn't see how the vampires had reached the bottom. There didn't seem to be any steps or even a ladder. He assumed they must have turned into bats and flown down.

The high priest rapped on the stone floor with his staff. "Let the purification begin!" he barked.

A low murmur went up from the vampires, a bass chant in a language Ben didn't recognize. The priest raised his voice above the chant and intoned some ancient prayer or incantation. The harsh syllables of a strange tongue poured from his mouth and echoed about the cenote. Ben wondered if this was the original Mayan language. Was the priest one of Camazotz's original vampires? Could he have been a man who had once lived and breathed when the mighty Mayan empire was at its peak? Watching the bizarre scene below, Ben found it easy to imagine the priest walking the streets of an ancient Mayan city, under the thrall of the demon god.

The vampires fell into a procession that passed by the brazier. As they reached it, some used the flames to light torches. The pit was soon filled with flickering firelight and thick black shadows that danced between the light from the flames.

When all the vampires had passed the brazier, they began to march around the temple, moving in rhythm to the words of the priest. They waved their torches across the carvings on the walls so that the stone monsters seemed to leap and dance weirdly in the shifting light, withdrawing into shadow as the torchbearers moved on. Ben found he was unable to look away from the strange sight. It was mesmerizing.

The procession ended when the vampires had circled the cenote, bathing the entire temple in firelight. As one, they turned to face the altar and the high priest.

"Let those who need the master's purification be brought forward!" the priest commanded.

The six vampires Ben had seen with the high priest

earlier now emerged from some unseen chamber behind the altar. They were dragging two unfortunate captives that Ben could not see clearly. He assumed they were human because they struggled in the vampires' clutches. Soon the humans were bound to the altar and the vampire priests withdrew.

For the first time, Ben could see the captives' faces, and he nearly cried aloud in shock and bewilderment. For, as he gazed down onto the altar slab below, he found himself looking at his sister and his best friend. Emily and Jack were the prisoners of the vampires.

CHAPTER SIXTEEN

Ben nearly leapt to his feet without thinking, but Edwin put a hand on his shoulder, to keep him down.

"It's just a purification," he murmured. "Not a sacrifice."

Emily and Jack were filthy, smeared with mud and grime. Ben couldn't imagine what they had been doing. They struggled, but their feet and hands were tied, and there was nothing they could do.

The high priest raised both hands and continued chanting. The other priests now took up the chant. Half singing, half wailing, they walked slowly around the altar, never taking their eyes off Emily and Jack. Sometimes the other vampires would respond to the chant. And it was always the same word that they said: *"Camazotz!"*

A priest walked forward. He daubed green and red paint first on Jack's face and forehead, then on Emily's.

"What are they doing?" Ben whispered.

"The temple needed purifying, and Emily and Jack are probably the reason why," Edwin whispered back. "They must have stumbled into this place somehow. Their presence has defiled it."

"Good on them," Ben murmured.

The chanting stopped suddenly. The high priest kept his hands held up to the sky and threw back his head. He screamed something in Mayan. Ben saw Edwin's lips move slowly as he tried to translate the words.

"I think," Edwin whispered, "that he said, 'The master is very near.'" He listened again as the high priest spoke once more, then he smiled with relief. "He also said, 'The temple is clean, the sacrifice is prepared, we await the master.' I think the sacrifice won't happen until Camazotz is here."

"It won't happen at all!" Ben hissed fiercely. Then he added, "How near is he?"

"Now, *that* he didn't say," Edwin replied. "Hang on, I think they're winding up down there."

Vampire priests moved forward and pulled Emily and Jack off the altar. The other vampires formed into a procession again. The captives were led to the middle of the troop, where they were closely guarded. The procession began to move toward the side of the cenote.

As the vampires started to climb the sides of the pit, Ben was astonished to see that there were steps after all. They were almost invisible, but there were stairs curved into the limestone wall of the cenote.

The vampires reached ground level some way from where Ben and Edwin were hiding. Ben tried to press himself flatter in the undergrowth in case any red eyes glanced in his direction, but none did. The procession made its way back into the jungle toward the village. Soon it was gone.

Ben suddenly realized that during the ceremony the jungle had fallen silent. Now that the vampires had moved away, the jungle's night chorus started up again, tentatively at first and then with more confidence. Within a few minutes it was as if the vampires had never come here.

"Well!" Edwin said quietly. "That was an experience."

Ben was on his feet. "We have to follow them!" he said. "We'll find out where they're keeping Em and Jack, and we'll rescue them."

But Edwin was shaking his head. "Not now," he said firmly. "Nothing is going to happen until Camazotz arrives, and there's nothing we can do against so many vampires. Remember what we came here for, Ben. We have to find the fourth piece of the amulet." He gestured toward the cenote. "It's down there somewhere and this might be our only chance to find it. *Then* we can go rescue Emily and Jack."

"But . . ." Ben began. But he knew Edwin was right, and so he sighed and nodded and followed his godfather to the far side of the cenote.

"They came up about here," Edwin said. His toes were right on the edge of the pit. Without the flaming torches below, it was just a pitch-black hole. "I don't think we'll make it down safely in the dark. We'll have to wait until sunup, when we can see the steps," he decided.

"Okay," Ben agreed. "So we'll search the temple at dawn and then we'll rescue Jack and Emily while it's still daylight."

Edwin nodded. "But first, we're spending the night in the jungle again," he said, and grinned. "It's better than that hut in the village, though, isn't it?"

The moment the sun peeked over the horizon the next morning, Ben and Edwin made their way down into the Lower Temple of Camazotz.

Even in daylight, the staircase was hard to see, so they felt their way down slowly, one step at a time. Against the towering walls of the cenote, Ben felt like an insect on the side of a mountain. Finally they both set foot at the bottom.

"The Lower Temple of Camazotz," Edwin murmured thoughtfully. He craned his head to look up and around. "It's completely unlike any of the other Mayan temples we know of, but it's perfect when you consider who Camazotz was — bat god of the underworld and all that. . . ."

Ben let his godfather talk. He was already exploring the temple, his blood-rose spear at the ready. It was broad daylight now, but the sun didn't reach all the way to the bottom of the pit — and that meant vampires could still walk around freely down here.

He passed the stone altar and stopped at the side of the pool. Close up, the water was very blue and clear. Behind the altar were other cave entrances — some natural openings, some that looked man-made. Ben supposed you couldn't have a temple without storerooms, meeting places, a chamber for the high priest, and so on. And it was all hidden away in the native rock of the Yucatán. "So, where is the moon piece going to be?" he asked.

"In the 'place of light' where no vampire would walk," Edwin replied, quoting Lorena and Emily's translation. "And definitely in the Lower Temple of Camazotz."

Ben looked around. "So, where is this 'place of light'?" he queried.

"Absolutely no idea," Edwin responded with his usual frankness. He was running his hand over some of the carvings on the wall. Ben had the feeling his godfather couldn't quite stop being an archaeologist even when he was also being a warrior against Camazotz.

"In the usual kind of temple, the place of light would probably be the top of the pyramid," Edwin continued. "But this isn't the usual kind of temple."

"The vampires may have found the moon piece already," Ben pointed out.

"They probably haven't, though, if they even know it's here at all," Edwin replied. "It was hidden after Camazotz was banished. And they won't have stumbled across it accidentally, if it's somewhere no vampire would walk." Edwin frowned. "Mind you, you have to admit that in a temple of Camazotz, there probably aren't many places where no vampire would walk. That should narrow our search a bit. I suggest we go our separate ways and try to find anywhere that could be the 'place of light.' Find that, and we've found the fourth piece of the amulet."

They started to explore the temple, each of them working his way around the base of the pit in opposite directions. Down here, the walls were covered in panels of hieroglyphs, tableaus of the gods, and sculptures of bats. Their wings, their eyes, and their teeth were square in the Mayan style, rather than round or curved in a more realistic manner, but the bats radiated a living, passionate hatred in a way Ben would not have thought possible with cold, dead rock.

He squinted up. The walls of the cenote sloped back slightly. At a height of about ten feet there was a small ridge, a walkway running all around the walls of the pit. Then there was another ten feet of carvings, then another walkway. The temple was like a very strange amphitheater, Ben thought. He could see that the carvings and the walkways went up for about forty feet before merging back into the native rough rock of the cenote. Above the final walkway, the walls were more or less vertical all the way to the top of the pit. Ben could see nothing that might be the "place of light."

By now, Ben had worked his way around to one of the cave mouths behind the altar. He thought it might be the one Emily and Jack had been dragged from the previous night. It was dark and unwelcoming. Ben held his blood-rose spear in front of him and edged forward cautiously. Dank air tickled his nostrils. He could make out dark walls on either side and even darker openings that seemed to lead to farther underground chambers. *There must be a maze of passages and tunnels back there*, he thought. Going on without a lamp of some kind didn't seem very sensible. He decided to head back to the light and thoroughly explore the parts of the temple he could see before he started on the parts he couldn't.

For the rest of the morning, Ben and Edwin thoroughly examined every inch of the lower areas of the temple without success. Then they began to work their way up the sides of the cenote and along each of the walkways.

It was shortly after noon when Ben paused to take a swig of water. He was up on the first walkway and he could see his godfather opposite him, making his way slowly around the same ridge.

As Ben let his gaze wander over the temple, he noticed something interesting. The sun had moved up higher in the sky, which meant its rays were reaching farther down the sides of the cenote. In fact, sunlight was just touching the highest of the walkways. Ben realized the sunlight must be spilling as far down into the temple as it ever did. It still didn't reach all the way to the bottom, but no vampire would go up onto that walkway in the direct sunlight. Ben felt a sudden surge of excitement. Could that walkway be the "place of light"?

The next moment, his excitement faded. If a vampire really wanted to walk up there, he realized, all it had to do was wait for the sun to go down.

Except that there was one part of the walkway that still wouldn't be accessible.

Ben stared more closely at the walls of the temple. His

attention was caught by one patch of sunlight that for some reason fell lower than any other. He glanced at the rim of the cenote and saw that there was a hollow up on the south side, a piece missing like a chip in the rim of a cup. It was this that let in the extra bit of light. The strange patch of sunlight shone on a section of rock that jutted out from the side of the cenote. Like everything else up there, it had been carved with pictures, and the fact that the rock stuck out from the wall made the carvings look much more three-dimensional than the rest. But the really significant thing was that the jutting rock completely blocked the topmost walk-way. No vampire would walk there, Ben thought, because it couldn't. There was nothing to walk on!

Edwin was at the other side of the cenote, peering closely at some statues. "Uncle Edwin!" Ben called eagerly.

Edwin hurried over. "Found something?" he inquired.

Ben gestured up at the rocky outcrop. "What's carved on that rock up there?" he asked curiously.

They both peered up at the carvings on the rock. They seemed to show Camazotz trampling someone else beneath his feet.

Edwin smiled. "That's Chac, being well and truly squashed by Camazotz, as far as I can tell," he explained. "Not quite how things worked out, of course—it was rather the other way around—but I expect it was carved before Camazotz's banishment."

"The vampires hate Chac," Ben said slowly.

"Oh, with a vengeance," Edwin agreed readily. "Now, if there's nothing else, Ben . . ." He started to walk away.

Ben reached for the side of the cenote and started to climb toward the outcrop of rock.

"Ben, what are you doing?" he heard Edwin ask after a moment.

"It's a carving that blocks the walkway," Ben called back. He kept climbing. "*And* it's in the sunlight, *and* it's carved with a picture of Chac. Do you think many vampires would go for a walk up there?"

There was a pause from below.

"You know, you could just use the steps," Edwin said. But the steps were all the way on the other side of the cenote, and after a few moments, Ben heard Edwin climbing up after him.

They scrambled their way up toward the top ridge, using the ancient carvings as toe- and handholds. It was farther away than it looked, and Ben was careful not to glance down at the stone floor of the temple in case he felt dizzy. But after a couple of minutes they were on the walkway, standing on either side of the jutting rock.

There was nothing there. Ben wasn't quite sure what he had expected—the fourth piece of the amulet sitting on top of the rock, perhaps hidden in a small hollow to conceal it from view? But of course, the crescent moon would have to have been more carefully hidden or it would have been found ages ago.

"Quite ingenious," Edwin muttered. He ran his hands over the carvings on the rock, poking and prying into every nook and cranny he could find. "How do you get a representation of your god into the temple of your enemy? You show him being defeated, of course! Is there anything on your side, Ben?"

Ben studied the rock more closely, squinting into every little hollow. He didn't enjoy being quite so close to Camazotz—even a Camazotz made of stone. The demon god was in his half-man, half-bat form and the carving made him about the same size as Ben himself. Chac was a much smaller, sadder figure beneath Camazotz's clawed feet. One arm seemed to be raised in futile defiance.

"Nothing," Ben reported sadly.

Edwin swore and thumped the stone with his fist. "It's always possible someone got here first, of course, but it doesn't seem very likely. If it was a European, we would probably have heard of this place and the piece would have ended up in a museum. If it was a local, the vampires would certainly have heard and come for the piece themselves."

"Unless," said Ben reluctantly, "this isn't the place the manuscript meant."

Edwin sighed heavily. "Perhaps it isn't. But if you can see somewhere else around here where no vampire would walk, feel free to point it out."

They slumped against the stone on either side of the outcrop, neither of them eager to climb back down again.

"Fantastic piece of art, though, isn't it?" Edwin remarked. Because they were both sitting down, they couldn't see each other. Ben could only hear his godfather's muffled voice from the other side of the rock. He thought Edwin's archaeological tendencies were emerging yet again.

"Never seen anything quite like it," Edwin continued. "Look how the sculptor has used the natural bumps of the rock to get the effect of muscles on Camazotz. And the carving spreads out. Look, it's going up the wall behind us, too."

Ben glanced casually over his shoulder. Now that Edwin mentioned it, he saw jagged streaks of raised rock running down the face of the cenote. They came from all directions, but they seemed to center on the rocky outcrop.

"I think it's lightning," said Ben. Now he realized why Chac had a hand raised. He was calling down his forces on his enemy. "Chac's defending himself." *And not very well*, he thought silently. One of the lightning bolts carved into the protruding rock was completely off course — it would miss Camazotz by a good foot.

"I think you're right," Edwin remarked after a moment. "Well, Chac, if you could give us a hand, we'd be eternally grateful."

Give us a hand! Ben thought with a wry smile. Chac's outstretched hand did seem to be offered to him. He frowned at it. Was it calling down lightning, or was it pointing? he wondered. And if it was pointing, what was it pointing at?

Ben shuffled along the ridge a bit so he could look back at where he had been sitting. All he could see was the off-course lightning bolt. Perhaps Chac was saying, *Oi, where do you think you're going?*

"Your master's calling you," Ben murmured to the streak of lightning. "He wants you over there." He idly punched the carving, as if to send it in the right direction, and it moved ever so slightly with the sound of stone grating on stone. A small trickle of dust and grit fell onto the ridge. Ben snatched his hand away.

"What was that?" Edwin's head appeared over the protruding rock.

"This . . ." Ben replied. He wriggled around onto his knees and put both hands against the carved stone. He pushed and again he felt that slight shift in the stone.

"Careful, Ben," Edwin said anxiously. "We don't want to destroy this valuable temple."

Ben personally could not have cared if the entire temple collapsed in on itself—provided they had recovered the crescent moon and got out before it did. He gave a third determined shove.

The lightning bolt slid aside, so that it was now striking down toward Camazotz—no longer off course. It left behind a small, dark space, and in the space Ben could see the gleam of gold.

"What do you see? What is it?" Edwin asked, leaning as far over the rock as he could.

Ben reached into the hole and felt cool, smooth metal under his fingers. He gripped it firmly and pulled the object out into the sunlight.

The crescent moon was six inches from tip to tip. The fourth piece of the amulet of Camazotz glittered a dull gold in the sunlight for the first time in a thousand years.

"That's it!" Edwin whispered in awe, his eyes shining. "Well done, Ben. Well done."

Ben handed it over without a second thought. "Put it in your bag," he said, "and let's rescue Em and Jack."

CHAPTER SEVENTEEN

Ben and Edwin crouched in the ruined barn where they had left the mules and peered out through the crack in the wall that they had used the previous night.

"So, where do you think they're keeping the prisoners?" Ben whispered. The place looked as silent and dead as it had the day before.

"They will be somewhere secure," Edwin replied, thinking aloud. "I doubt this place has a town jail, so Emily and Jack must be somewhere else that can be locked up."

"They could be in any of the huts," Ben pointed out, "with a couple of vampire guards."

"They could," Edwin agreed, "but even vampires need sleep. And guards would only have to make one mistake and Jack and Emily might escape and get out into the sunlight where they'd be safe. No, it's more likely they'll be under lock and key."

Ben picked at a crumbling fragment of the wall next to him. "Most of these buildings are falling apart. Given a whole day, Jack and Emily could probably dig their way out."

"I expect that will have occurred to their captors,"

Edwin mused. Then he smiled. "Of course! They're probably underground."

Ben groaned. "Not again!"

"Oh, no, no," Edwin said. "I'm not talking about caves this time. But some of these huts must have cellars— somewhere the original villagers could store food without it spoiling in the heat. We have to find those huts. Come on." He got up and hurried out into the sunlight.

Ben followed. It was an odd feeling, walking around the village and knowing that vampires lurked in some of the buildings. He knew the vampires couldn't come out into the sunlight, but they could still shout a warning to one another. He and Edwin had to be careful they weren't spotted.

Fortunately most of the huts could be quickly crossed off the list. As Ben had noticed the day before, they stood on little stilts with crawlspaces beneath. It was obvious that none of those had cellars.

That left only a handful. Ben and Edwin crept among them, always keeping low, always checking to see which windows had a view of them. They only moved when they were certain there were no vampires to see them. And hut by hut, they gradually narrowed their search. Some of the likely-looking buildings were obviously empty; the doors stood ajar or weren't there at all. Still, Ben and Edwin checked inside them to see if there was any kind of underground entrance.

Finally there were just two huts left. One had its door

firmly closed. They carefully pressed their ears to the wood and listened. There was no sound at all from within. They looked at each other and nodded. Then, blood-rose spears in hand, they threw the door open and leapt inside.

The hut was empty, save for a few pieces of furniture. There were no vampires and no trapdoors set into the ground that might lead to a cellar.

That left just one hut, and this one certainly seemed promising. It had a good, sturdy door, which was firmly locked with a slightly rusty but very solid padlock.

A padlock! Ben stared at it in frustration. He and Edwin had blood rose — they could handle vampires. But a simple padlock was a problem.

The hut was on one side of the village. Edwin led Ben quietly around the back, out of sight of other buildings. "It has to be this one," Edwin whispered.

"Jack could probably pick that lock," Ben said bitterly. "Can you? I know I can't."

Edwin shook his head. "We could probably look around for some kind of lever, something to break it with . . . but, no. Much too noisy. If there's a guard in there he would be alerted at once."

Ben sighed and looked around for inspiration. Thoughtfully he reached up over his head. He found he could just touch the top of the hut wall and the wooden framework that supported the thatched roof. The ends of the struts that made up the frame poked out from beneath the thatch. He put a hand on one strut, then his other hand on the one next to it. He brought his hands down and looked at the gap between them. It was just wider than he was.

"How thick is the thatch on the roof?" he asked quietly.

Edwin shrugged. "No more than an inch or two, I expect," he said.

"Could it hold my weight?"

"I doubt it. You'd go straight through. . . ." Edwin suddenly realized what Ben had in mind. "Brilliant!" he hissed. "I'll give you a leg up."

"Hang on," Ben said, and carefully detached a sprig of blood rose from his spear. He tried to put it into a pocket, but the thorns came straight through the cloth and scratched his leg. So he tucked it into the folds of his rolled-up shirtsleeve. "Up we go, then!"

Edwin put his hands together and bent to give Ben support. Ben clambered up, first onto Edwin's shoulders and then onto the top of the wall. His toes accidentally kicked against the mud bricks as he lifted his foot off Edwin's shoulders. He carefully plucked the blood rose from his shirtsleeve and took a firm hold on it. He had thought carefully about the next part, but there was no way of doing it quietly. So he took a breath and leapt forward.

Ben's weight carried him through the thatch as if it weren't there. There was a horrible sensation of falling, and the thatch scratched his face. But then he was inside the hut. Unfortunately his right foot hit a chair as he landed, while his left foot kept going. Ben toppled over in midair, arms flailing, and slammed into the dirt floor with a thud that knocked the breath from his body.

If there had been any vampires in the hut, he would probably have died there and then. The blood rose had fallen from his hand and he was too winded to defend himself anyway. But the hut was empty. He lay there and groaned.

"Ben! *Ben!* Are you all right?" Edwin was whispering anxiously from the other side of the wall.

Ben groaned, rolled over, and climbed to his feet. "Yes," he replied. "Never better."

He staggered and leaned against the wall, taking in his surroundings. The door was locked, the windows were shuttered—it was very dark and gloomy. Ben could just make out some tattered furniture, pots and pans by the fireplace, and a wooden trapdoor set into the floor.

Thankfully this wasn't padlocked, but there was a thick plank of wood jammed through the twin handles so that it couldn't be opened from below. Ben picked his blood rose up from the floor—just in case—and held it at the ready. With his free hand he pulled the plank out and opened the trapdoor.

Jack and Emily erupted from the ground, two shadowy figures that cannoned into Ben and knocked him flat. Ben found himself lying on his back with Jack astride him.

"Quick, Emily, quick!" Jack shouted, the fingers of one hand wrapped tight around Ben's neck, his other hand drawn back to deliver a colossal punch.

Emily had a broken chair leg clasped in both hands. She was poised to swing it down onto Ben's head.

"Em . . ." Ben croaked. "Jack . . ."

The chair leg and Jack's clenched fist stopped inches from Ben's face. Jack peered down at his rescuer through the gloom. "Hey, Emily! Look who turned up."

"Ben!" Emily and Jack pulled Ben to his feet, and Emily gave him a hug.

"Sorry about the little misunderstanding, mate," said Jack.

"We thought we'd try a getaway if we could," Emily explained. "Anything's better than what they've got planned for us."

"They're going to sacrifice us to Big Ugly when he gets here," Jack explained.

"I know," Ben said. He tucked the blood rose back into his sleeve. "I saw you in the temple."

"I ain't even going to ask how you got here," Jack said.

Ben smiled back. "And I'm not going to ask how *you* did, either. At least not right now. Uncle Edwin's outside, and we've found the crescent moon of the amulet, so let's go!"

The only way out was Ben's way in. At least his method of entry had left a convenient gap that the others could climb through. They sent Emily first. Jack insisted on going last so he could push Ben up, and Ben was grateful because he was still sore and wasn't certain he could pull himself up on his own. Outside, on the ground, Emily and Edwin were waiting for him. Ben gingerly let himself down, and then Jack leapt nimbly after him.

In the bright sunlight, Jack and Emily looked even more grubby than when Ben had last seen them. They had done their best to rub off the paint from the purification ritual, and there were red and green smudges all over their faces and their clothes.

Edwin led them all back to the barn where they had left the mules. They left the village as fast as the animals would carry them.

As they plunged into the jungle, they exchanged stories. Edwin and Emily rode one mule, Ben and Jack the other. It was the first time Edwin and Ben had heard about the fate of the Brotherhood's army, or Lorena's treachery, or Roberto's valiant sacrifice.

"So, most of the Brotherhood of Chac are *gone*?" Edwin asked incredulously.

Jack nodded.

Edwin shook his head and looked away, unable to speak about the tragedy.

"Camazotz will come for the moon," Ben pointed out. "It won't be hard for him to work out who found it. And we're going to need an army to defend ourselves."

"At least we've escaped," Emily put in.

"For the moment," Edwin said grimly. He glanced up at the sky. Searching the village for the hut with the cellar had taken up more of the day than he would have liked. "We have a couple of hours of sunlight left," he continued. "Which means that in a couple of hours, we four are going to become the most hunted beings on the face of the planet."

Suddenly they were interrupted by a European voice, speaking out of the shadows. "Who is there?" it demanded imperiously.

It was utterly unexpected. Edwin and Ben hurriedly reined in their mules as figures loomed out of the undergrowth in front of them.

The newcomers were tall and slim, not at all like the native Mayans. Their tall hats and long cloaks indicated that they were European, and their white faces showed pale in the shadowy jungle depths.

Ben could hardly believe his eyes. The men looked so incongruous here in the rain forest. But then he remembered that he and Edwin had looked like that once — on the original expedition. This could only be another expedition, he thought, run by Europeans who stuck to their traditional dress, however ridiculous they looked.

"And who are you?" asked Edwin cautiously.

But Ben interrupted. "Please, that's not important!" he said urgently. "You have to leave here right away. We're all in terrible danger if we don't—"

"Terrible danger?" asked another voice.

Ben was flooded by a sudden, sick dread. The figures parted in front of him and one man stepped forward. Ben knew him instantly. He also remembered—too late, much too late—how the vampires had always been able to walk around beneath the leafy canopy, even during the day, provided no direct sunlight fell on their skin.

The jungle had fallen quiet. Not a cheep, not a squawk, not a single sound from any living thing broke the silence. And Ben stared at the Vicomte de Montargis. The man's hair and his short silver beard were as neatly trimmed as ever, but he no longer wore spectacles. Their gazes locked. The vicomte's eyes, once warm and human, now began to burn with an evil red flame.

"My dear Cole," said Camazotz, "I've never felt safer."

CHAPTER EIGHTEEN

Camazotz had finally returned to the jungle.

Ben hauled quickly on the mule's reins to wheel it around, but other red-eyed figures were appearing behind them. They were surrounded. There was nowhere to run.

Camazotz stepped forward and looked up at Edwin. "Sherwood," he said thoughtfully. "You are just full of surprises."

Edwin was staring at him in horror. "Dear God," he murmured.

Camazotz suddenly held up a hand. The gesture was so commanding that even Edwin fell silent. A look of awe and greed crossed the demon god's face. "The crescent moon. It is near," he breathed. "I sense it . . . here!" He reached out for Edwin's saddlebag.

With an angry cry, Edwin slashed at him with his blood rose.

Camazotz's hand moved too quickly for anyone to see. He grasped Edwin's wrist and twisted, hauling him off the mule. Edwin shouted with pain as he fell. He hit the ground and lay there, writing in agony. Emily leapt off the mule to help him.

Camazotz reached into the saddlebag. His eyes blazed with unholy joy as he pulled out the fourth piece of the amulet.

Ben thought that the curve of the crescent moon looked like a cruel smile, mocking everything they had done to try to defeat the vampire god of the Maya. He shut his eyes in despair and felt Jack slump against him. They had failed. They had sworn they would not let Camazotz get the final piece of the amulet, and now he had it. He had them. He had everything.

"How appropriate," Camazotz chuckled. "The means of my ultimate power, delivered into my hands by the enemies who swore to destroy me." He stretched out a hand over Edwin's head, as if sensing something.

"Two bites," he murmured. "One more and you are my servant forever. . . ."

Edwin shuddered and Emily tightened her arms around him protectively.

"But no," Camazotz said suddenly. "I have need of you. I have need of you all." The demon god raised his voice to address his servants. "Leave the animals. Camazotz does not ride on beasts of burden!" He turned back to Ben and his friends. "You four will walk to my temple," he said, smiling. "And then you will finally see the might and the glory of Camazotz."

"Strange sense of . . . what's that word?" Jack said. "Means you seen it before?"

"Déjà vu," replied Ben, Edwin, and Emily together.

"Yeah, that," Jack agreed. "They kept us here last night," he added, by way of explanation for Ben and Edwin.

They were back in the temple at the bottom of the cenote. The vampires had escorted their master to the village, where they had met the local vampires hurrying in the opposite direction, in pursuit of their escaped captives. It had been like the triumphant return of a hero. The shrieks and hisses of delight must have been heard for miles around. Flocks of bats wheeled overhead in celebration. The friends had been surrounded by an endless sea of rejoicing vampires.

Edwin had been in agony every step of the way. Camazotz had dislocated his shoulder and none of the friends knew how to repair the damage. Emily had had to bind Edwin's arm as they walked, using one of his torn-off shirtsleeves as a bandage.

Finally they had reached the temple and the four of them had been confined in a cave off to one side of the stone platform and the pool. They had been there ever since. The hours had passed slowly.

There was no door to the cave, just a pair of vampires guarding the other side of the entrance. And beyond them, a few hundred more. The sounds of their revelry echoed through the stone.

"I don't understand," Edwin muttered through clenched teeth. "Why didn't he just slaughter us there and then? Why this insane desire to gloat?"

The three friends looked at one another.

"He's got something in mind," Jack said, remembering the last time they had come face-to-face with Camazotz.

Ben apparently remembered, too. "In Paris, he mentioned a ritual that would consolidate his power forever," he explained. "It involved beating hearts."

"Ah." Edwin drew in his breath with a shudder. "I wish I hadn't asked."

"Don't worry, Uncle Edwin," Emily said with a wry smile. "If we remember any more cheerful news, we won't hesitate to keep it to ourselves."

A vampire appeared in the entrance to the cave. He was in human form and he looked like a Mayan peasant. Other vampires waited behind him.

"It is time. The master summons you," said the first.

Edwin sighed. "Help me up, will you?"

The three friends helped him to his feet. And before any of them could say or do anything else, the vampires came forward and bundled them roughly out of the cave.

"Can't keep His Toothiness waiting, can we?" Jack said as he was pushed out into the open.

The temple was a riot of vampire festivities. Hideous,

twisted parodies of living beings capered and cavorted like monstrous children at a party in Hell. But a silence gradually spread over the throng as the captives emerged into the torchlight and were led to the altar.

Then the crowd parted and Camazotz himself approached. He was no longer dressed as a European. Instead he wore a long cloak of feathers edged with shrunken human skulls. A massive golden breastplate in the shape of a snarling bat's head covered his chest. Even though his form was still that of the Vicomte de Montargis, there was no doubt that Camazotz the god had returned to his old realm and his old powers.

Jack noticed that Camazotz's eyes were burning orbs of fire that distorted the rest of his face, making it hard to see his features. In a strange way, Jack felt glad. It was better not to see the face of his old friend the vicomte inhabited by this demon.

Camazotz's mouth twisted in a cruel smile. "Release them," he said. "They have nowhere to run."

The vampires released the four friends, who stood side by side next to the altar stone. Camazotz gestured and his high priest stepped forward, carrying a small wooden table. The table was covered with a red silk cloth. Laid out on the cloth were the four pieces of the amulet.

It was the first time the friends had seen all four together. They were arranged in a circle. Clockwise, Jack saw the eye, the bat, the crown, and the moon. There was about an inch between each one.

The priest reverently set the table down between the captives and his master. He bowed and backed away.

"My amulet," Camazotz hissed in delight. "At last." He stared at the friends. "And despite your best efforts to prevent this moment, today will change the history of your world."

Jack swallowed and took a breath. He might be about to die, but he had no intention of letting Camazotz have the last word. "Maybe it will," he said. "Maybe darkness will come over the world. But there'll still be blood rose, and homes you can't enter, and people who will fight back. It's not over yet."

For a moment Camazotz almost looked surprised. "You *are* well informed," he remarked. "You must have read those parchments carefully." He ran his fingers greedily over the golden pieces of the amulet. His voice was almost conversational. "But you are not well informed *enough*, boy," he continued. "Darkness alone will not confirm my rule forever, it is true. But there is another ritual I can perform once the amulet is complete. I simply pour the fresh heart's blood of a different human over each piece. And then . . ." He towered over the friends, and his eyes burned even more brightly. "*Then*, there will be no barrier that can stand against my power. Blood rose will be no more than an ugly weed and no private home will be closed to my vampires. There will be nowhere in or under this world that your race can hide. We will hunt you, we will drink your blood, and we will rule supreme." His voice grew deeper and louder as he spoke, and Jack heard the first rumbling echo of Camazotz's natural voice.

And then Camazotz glanced up suddenly and the friends inadvertently followed his gaze. The vampires did likewise, and gasped. A faint orange light licked the rim of the cenote.

"Sunrise," said Camazotz with deep satisfaction. "It is time."

He stepped aside abruptly and barked an order in Mayan. The high priest came forward and bowed deeply to his god. Then he turned to the friends, his eyes gleaming.

Strong hands suddenly grasped them from behind. Jack had been so intent on watching the priest that he hadn't noticed the other vampires. Clawlike hands closed around his arms, and though he struggled, he couldn't escape. Out of the corner of his eye he could see his friends restrained in the same way.

The high priest held up a knife and advanced. The blade was sharp black stone, two feet long and gleaming. The priest approached Jack.

This is it, Jack thought despairingly, *this is finally it*. He squeezed his eyes shut so that he wouldn't have to watch, and he steeled himself so that he wouldn't flinch when the blade cut in.

Unexpectedly a strong hand seized his arm. It felt like a red-hot wire running down his wrist. Jack opened his eyes again. The priest had simply opened a two-inch cut in his arm. Blood flowed freely and one of the priest's acolytes ran forward with a bowl to collect it.

"We only need your blood at this stage," Camazotz said,

sounding amused. "The pieces of the amulet must be prepared before we take your hearts."

The vampire holding Jack released him, and Jack clutched his arm to his chest, pressing the wound against his shirt, while the high priest repeated the process on Emily, Ben, and Edwin.

When the blood of all four friends had been collected in four separate bowls, the acolytes held out the bowls, and the high priest began to chant. He took a feather from Camazotz's cloak and dipped it into the first bowl of blood. Then he began to walk around the table, sprinkling Jack's blood on the bat section of the amulet.

The vampires were completely silent, but Jack felt a growing power in the air of the temple. He remembered when they had brewed the potion to banish Camazotz in Professor Adensnap's kitchen. There had been a similar atmosphere then—a sense of great forces gathering in a small place. But those had been forces of light, of radiance, of *good*. These forces served Camazotz.

The high priest took another feather and moved to the next bowl. Emily's blood was sprinkled on the eye section, Ben's on the crown, and Edwin's on the crescent moon. Finally the priest laid down the feathers and moved the eye and the bat sections of the amulet together.

A wave of darkness rippled out and up to meet the sunrise.

Jack gasped, and a murmur of appreciation and glee went up from the vampires.

Another wave flowed out to follow the first. It rose up the cenote like a giant ring of mist.

Was the sky up above slightly darker? Jack wondered. He didn't see how it could be. He had always thought that darkness was just the absence of light. It wasn't a *thing* that someone could create. But apparently, in the realm of Camazotz, it was!

Camazotz laughed. The sound echoed around the underground temple, and his voice grew deeper. He sounded less and less like the vicomte of old and more and more like the hell-born demon that he was. *"It begins, my servants! It begins!"* he cried in delight.

The priest began to walk around the amulet, chanting again. The sense of power grew. To Jack, the air seemed charged with darkness. It was almost a physical pressure upon him—like waiting for a thunderstorm that would not break.

Again the priest reached out for the pieces of the amulet, and this time he slotted the crown into the feet of the bat. Darkness shot up from the three joined pieces like a fountain.

Jack watched in an agony of suspense. And that was when the idea came to him. There wasn't time to think it through, and besides, he had a horrible feeling at the back of his mind that if he thought about it too long, he would lose his nerve. Instead he stepped forward toward the table and the amulet.

"You think you're so clever?" he shouted at Camazotz. "You think your toy will change things? But you're wrong!"

The vampires hissed in anger.

Camazotz bellowed with rage. *"Stand back from the amulet!"*

"Oh, that?" Jack gave a dismissive wave as if the amulet were just a trinket—a child's plaything of no importance. "What difference does that make?" He took another step forward. "Go ahead, put it all together. Make it dark everywhere. But I tell you this," he went on, taking one more step, "there's four of us here, but millions and millions to stand against you out there. Your Mayan empire weren't nothing compared to what we got now. So go on, Camazotz, put your little toy together. Get your vampire servants to do it, 'cos you'll never make us do anything we don't want to!"

Camazotz roared, a sound that could have come from no human throat. The sheer pressure of his voice made Jack step back.

"Impudence!" Camazotz snarled. But then he started to laugh again. His whole body shook. His whole body *rippled*. His form was changing, growing. *"You have the nerve to face me in my most sacred place of power and tell me my empire was nothing? You miserable little worm!"* he cried. Then he laughed again. *"You will be rewarded for your impertinence, boy. I had planned to keep the Cole boy for last, but he at least has the sense to stay quiet now. You will be the last to die. You will see*

the hearts of your friends crushed over my amulet to give me my full power!"

Camazotz gestured at Ben, who had been watching Jack's defiance openmouthed. *"Take that boy away and bring me his heart!"* he commanded.

"No!" Emily screamed.

But four vampires stepped forward and grabbed hold of Ben. And though he fought and struggled, the hands that held him were just too strong.

"Stay brave, Em!" he shouted as they dragged him away. "Jack's right! Camazotz's a sad, pathetic, cowardly, bullying . . ."

The laughter of Camazotz echoed off the rock walls, drowning out Ben's last words as the vampires pulled him back inside the temple.

Jack just had time for one horrified thought: *It weren't meant to go like that!* And then Camazotz's powers of mind control invaded his head, forcing him to turn to look at the vampire god.

Jack recoiled in horror. "No! Oh, no!" he gasped. For the monster that loomed over him was like nothing Jack had ever seen. He felt unutterable terror. How could they ever fight this creature? he wondered. For this was a demon, evil beyond measure—but also a god!

The vicomte's human body was gone. In its place stood Camazotz—revealed at last in all the horrifying might and majesty of his natural form.

CHAPTER NINETEEN

Emily stared up at Camazotz as he towered above them, taller than any mortal man. His skin was gray as ash, cracked and split by hellfire and the passing of centuries. Demon horns jutted from his head and bat's ears twisted toward the captives like the ears of a cat pointing at a mouse. Where his eyes should be, twin globes of fire were set into his skull. His tail lashed the stone floor like a whip.

He flexed his shoulders and two enormous bat wings unfolded from his back with a sound like shredding timber. They flapped and a gale of hot, rancid air blew against the friends.

Camazotz fixed his eyes on Emily, Edwin, and Jack. *"Kneel,"* he commanded them. *"Kneel before your god!"*

Despair flooded Emily. Her tears still flowed for Ben and his fate, but she blinked them back and made herself replace sorrow with fury and hatred of Camazotz. But again, she felt the irresistible power of Camazotz inside her head, making her do what she did not want to do, trying to force her to her knees.

With a cry of pure misery, Edwin fell to his knees beside

her. He stayed there, on the floor, his head hung in shame. He had been so weakened by his injury, Emily thought, he was not able to resist. She staggered as the pressure of Camazotz's will almost became too much. But she was young and strong, like Jack. She resolved she would *not* bow down. She would fight. . . .

And then a memory came to her, unbidden, out of nowhere. There was a chant. What had the words been? Ben had mentioned them.

Come on, Emily! she chided herself as she felt her legs buckling. *You're the one who's good with words!*

"*L-lah* . . ." she began hesitantly, and for a fraction of a second, she could have sworn Camazotz's grip on her weakened.

"*Lah yich saknik, maknik Chac!*" she shouted as the words came flooding back. It was the chant that Roberto had taught Jack and Ben. The chant that freed the minds of men from the grasp of Camazotz.

Immediately the bonds that held her vanished. But only for a moment, and then the pressure was suddenly back — stronger than before.

"*Kneel!*" Camazotz raged.

"*Lah yich saknik, maknik Chac!*" Emily gasped.

"*KNEEL!*"

"*Lah yich saknik* . . ." Blood roared in her ears and her head felt as if it would burst under the strain. She dimly heard Jack's voice joining in, mumbling the same words over and over. It helped, but still the power of Camazotz grew in her head. Despair began to creep back in. What could she do? She was one girl. She wasn't strong enough to fight a god.

But, to her astonishment, it was Jack who cracked first. He screamed once, long and loud, and then threw himself sobbing onto the ground before Camazotz. "I can't do it!" he sobbed. "I can't fight you! You're too powerful. None of us can. . . ."

A murmur of glee went up from the crowd of vampires, and again Camazotz's grip vanished from Emily's mind. But she was so horrified she barely noticed.

"Oh, Jack," she whispered, "please, no . . ."

Jack turned a tear-streaked face toward her. "I'm sorry, Emily. But you know we can't do it, we can't defeat the master, he's too strong." He turned back to Camazotz. "Forgive me, master, forgive me. I beg you, spare me. . . ." His whole body heaved with sobs.

"*Finally!*" Camazotz's voice crawled with a loathsome satisfaction.

Emily closed her eyes. She wanted to weep. It was almost worse than seeing Ben dragged off to his death. Jack—brave, strong, noble Jack—was reduced to this weeping, groveling huddle.

When she opened her eyes again, she saw that Jack had crawled forward and was now slumped against the leathery, repulsive skin of Camazotz's leg. He looked like a small child pathetically begging for comfort from an adult.

Camazotz looked down sternly. "*You know there can be*

no forgiveness for the crimes you have committed against me," he said.

Jack turned his tearstained face up to Camazotz. "Please, master, please . . ." he whimpered.

"*Put the last piece of the amulet into place, and I promise your death will be swift and painless,*" Camazotz declared.

Jack bit his lip and looked down. Another fit of sobbing racked his body, but then he nodded and crawled toward the table.

Camazotz gestured at the high priest—who had stopped performing the ritual when Jack first stepped forward—and he moved aside.

Emily watched Jack reach for the pieces of the amulet and felt her heart breaking.

But then Ben's voice echoed around the pit. "Jack! No!"

Emily's head whipped around. Jack looked up in astonishment. Ben was charging toward them. His shirt was ripped, but otherwise he seemed unhurt. He vaulted over the altar stone and hurled himself at his friend. A vampire screeched in rage and stepped into his path. Ben slashed at it with a sprig of blood rose and the vampire crumbled into ash.

And then Ben knocked into Jack, sending him flying. Jack scrambled to his feet and threw himself at Ben, wrapping his arms around his waist and driving him back. Ben slammed into the altar and the blood rose fell to the floor. Emily saw Camazotz gesture at it, and the plant flared briefly into flame before dissolving into ash like the vampire before it.

Jack and Ben were locked in combat, their arms tight around each other, staggering across the temple. Jack brought his knee up into Ben's stomach, and Ben doubled over with a gasp as the air was driven from his lungs. Jack clubbed him on the back of the head and Ben fell to his knees.

"Jack!" Emily screamed. "Stop it! He's your *friend*!"

Jack glanced at her for a split second, and Emily saw that his face was dead and cold. Then he turned back to Ben and lashed out with his foot, catching Ben in the stomach. Ben cried out and fell flat to the ground, groaning. Jack kicked him again and Emily saw her brother slump into stillness.

Instantly Jack turned away and moved briskly back to the table. He bowed to Camazotz and then took hold of the final piece of the amulet—the crescent moon. His hands moved swiftly over the pieces, and then he stepped back. "It is done, master," he said.

CHAPTER TWENTY

"No! Jack, no!" Emily barely heard her own scream. Her eyes were fixed on the amulet, waiting for darkness to billow out and smother the world.

She was dimly aware of Jack, her best-friend-turned-traitor, standing before Camazotz with his head bowed in submission. Of Edwin, staring in horror and disbelief. Of Ben, who was groggily pushing himself up and looking around in bewilderment.

The delighted murmur of the vampires and the laughter of Camazotz were louder than ever. The army of the demon god knew that nothing could stop them now.

Then a lightning bolt shot out of the amulet. It scythed into the crowd of vampires and a cluster of them simply disappeared in a cloud of ash. Their laughter turned to screams of panic and confusion. Another lightning bolt blazed into another corner of the temple. The vampires threw themselves out of its way, but some were too slow and they went the way of their brothers.

"*NO!*" Camazotz roared. "*NO! IT CANNOT BE!*"

And then the amulet erupted in lightning. Tendrils of

shining, crackling energy shot out in all directions. Emily felt one go straight through her. It tingled with power.

The screeching vampires were hemmed in by the sides of the temple. There was only one escape. As one, they shifted into bat form and took flight. In a matter of moments, the air was black with vampire bats.

It was only a temporary escape. The creatures were caught between the treacherous amulet below and the sunrise above. Some chose the sunlight as the lesser threat and flew straight into it. They had exploded into ash by the time they reached the rim of the cenote. Others were picked off, dozens of them at a time, by lightning from the amulet.

Emily looked around her. Camazotz was howling in fury. Jack, Ben, and Edwin were staring at the massacre of the vampires, transfixed by the scene before them. They didn't see the priest, one of the few vampires as yet untouched by the lightning, lunging at the amulet. But Emily did.

"Oh, no, you don't!" she shouted, and threw herself at him. She hit him just before he reached the amulet's table, and he was knocked to the floor. He snarled and turned his hands into claws to slash at Emily's throat. But then, blessedly, a lightning bolt impaled him and he vanished in a cloud of swirling ash. Emily coughed and choked, waving her hands in front of her.

"Chac!" Camazotz hissed furiously, and he strode forward, reaching out for the amulet himself.

And with that, the full energy of the complete amulet

burned into him with a searing white light that was too painful to look at. Camazotz screamed, transfixed by the lightning. His skin split open in a thousand cracks. Pure white energy blazed from the wounds.

His form collapsed into something much smaller, and Emily recognized the figure of the vicomte, which shifted to become Sir Donald Finlay, then a man she didn't recognize—a Mayan, to judge by his look. And another. And another. All the forms that Camazotz had ever taken—all the men whose bodies and lives he had stolen so that he himself might have human shape—their figures flashed before Emily now.

And then there was a final blaze of light, an explosion, and Camazotz disintegrated into a million blazing pieces that burned brightly, then vanished.

The air was clean. Even the ash was gone. There was no sign of the vampires or of Camazotz. A strange noise drifted down gently from above. Or rather, Emily thought, it was not strange, but they hadn't heard it for hours—the birds of the jungle were singing again. Emily gazed upward and saw sunlight—real, clean sunlight, unpolluted by the darkness from the amulet.

It was over.

Jack and Ben stood in front of Emily. She blinked uncertainly up at them, still dazed by what had happened. They were both smiling happily, and Ben didn't seem injured at all.

Jack held out his hands to help her up. "Eye, moon,

crown, bat, right?" Jack said. "The *other* way to assemble the amulet?"

Jack seemed his old self again. So Emily let him pull her to her feet. "You're . . . It was a trick?" she whispered uncertainly as the truth dawned on her. "But it seemed so real. You were *crying*!"

Jack looked at her innocently, and suddenly his face crumpled and tears welled up in his eyes. "Please, missus!" he sobbed. "Me mum's so ill, she ain't eating anything and she can't go out to work, and there's five of us to feed. I just need a shilling, missus, please, just a shilling to see us all through another night. . . ." He rubbed his arm across his eyes and suddenly his playful grin was back. "Nothing to it," he said. "I've had to rely on that trick more than once in my time. I were afraid I might be out of practice, though."

Emily stared at Jack in amazement.

"Jack is very clever and very brave," said Edwin, who was still kneeling on the ground. His voice sounded weak. "Could you possibly help me up as well?"

Jack and Emily moved quickly to his side.

"Wait there a moment," Ben said, and hurried away.

"But . . . Ben!" Emily called. "What happened to *you*?"

Ben had disappeared back into the cave from which he had emerged. Emily and Jack looked at each other and shrugged as they helped Edwin to his feet.

"This is what happened to me," Ben said a moment later. He came around the corner with a huge smile on his face, struggling under the weight of . . .

"Roberto!" Jack and Emily exclaimed together. Their friend managed to smile back at them.

"Well, well," said Edwin, grinning and cradling his injured arm. "We are the walking wounded, aren't we?"

"They took me into that cave," Ben said. "And tore my shirt open. Then they were about to cut my heart out when I decided it was time to use my blood rose."

"Blood rose?" Emily repeated. "Where was that?" She looked him up and down, trying to see where he could have hidden it.

"Here," he said, patting his sleeve. "I've had it there ever since I climbed through the roof to rescue you. When they caught us in the jungle, I couldn't really use it against so many vampires, but when it was life or death . . ." He shrugged. "Anyway, I got a couple of them. But then one grabbed my hand and held it, and the other came at me with a knife. And then, in the nick of time, Roberto sneaked up behind them and stabbed them both with blood rose."

"I had time to recover a little," Roberto explained. "So I followed after you."

"Through the pool?" Jack asked.

Roberto frowned. "There was a pool? No. I followed the sound of the vampires, and it led me to a way out. I thought I could sit there in the dark and die quietly, or I could die facing my people's ancient enemy. I came out into the cave just as they were fighting Ben."

"And Ben darn near spoiled everything," Jack said with feeling, "till I managed to tell him it were all a trick while

180

we was fighting. You don't pull your punches, mate." He rubbed his jaw ruefully. Emily could see a bruise developing there.

Ben laughed and shook his head.

"It was a dangerous game, Jack," Edwin commented.

Jack shrugged. "Couldn't think of another way he'd let us close to the amulet. All that about us not doing anything we didn't want to—well, I was hoping Camazotz would prove his point by making me put the amulet together. And then I'd put the pieces into the wrong order for him. Um . . ." He glanced at Ben in embarrassment. "Weren't planning on him cutting your heart out, though. Sorry about that."

Ben grinned and patted his chest. "It's still here, and with a bit of luck, it's going to keep beating until I reach a fine old age."

"And it's over," Emily said. "Please say it's over!"

Roberto smiled and nodded. "It is over."

"And we have marvelous archaeological treasures to show for it!" Edwin added.

The others groaned.

He ignored them. "There's the amulet. . . ." They all looked at the place where it had been. Splashes of melted gold among the charred fragments of the table were all that remained of the amulet.

"Ah, well," said Edwin. "We still have this temple, unique and unprecedented."

"You're not serious!" Jack exclaimed. "This were the

Lower Temple of Camazotz! Hundreds of people died here. And you want to keep it? You can't mean it!"

"No," said Ben, smiling. "He doesn't."

"Ah, Ben, you read me too well," Edwin said with a laugh. "Roberto, does the Brotherhood of Chac own any supplies of gunpowder?"

"We have two or three barrels, yes," Roberto told him.

Edwin nodded and looked around. "Two or three barrels," he said. "Yes. That should do it."

EPILOGUE

"We will hide the Temple of Camazotz forever," Roberto said cheerfully. The friends stood on the coast, their backs to the sea, the cool breeze ruffling their hair. Their experiences in the cenote already seemed a lifetime ago.

They had not been looking forward to the journey back through the jungle. Roberto and Edwin were still wounded, though Roberto's arms were strong and he was able to put Edwin's shoulder back into position with a sudden wrench and a lot of pain. The rain forest was as hot and oppressive as ever, and there was a long way to go.

But almost the first things they saw when they walked back through the village were the mules that Camazotz had abandoned. The faithful animals had made their own way after them. And with the mules, the journey became much easier. The friends traveled by day and slept openly by night. The usual jungle chorus of barks, howls, and squawks accompanied them all the way, and the only bloodsuckers around were mosquitoes. The journey was almost pleasant.

On the third day, they made it back to camp. The remaining members of the Brotherhood of Chac had learned what had happened to their comrades. They had assumed that the three friends, Edwin, and Roberto had met the same fate, so there was great rejoicing when they heard the news about Camazotz. But the heroes felt too weary to join in. The first order of business had been a good meal, baths all around, and a long, long sleep.

Now a little skiff waited to carry Edwin, Jack, Ben, and Emily out to the Brotherhood's ship. It would take them back across the Gulf of Mexico to New Orleans, and from there they would make their way back home to London.

"Still, losing the temple does seem a shame," Edwin said, and recoiled under a barrage of scowls and groans. "Joking, joking," he said hurriedly.

Emily kissed Roberto. "Thank you for everything," she said.

Jack and Ben shook his hand.

"Thanks for being a good shot," said Ben.

"Couldn't have done it without you, mate," Jack added.

Roberto's face was a large smile. "*I* should be thanking *you*," he told them. "You have lifted a terrible curse from our land. There should be statues in your honor, but you return to England where no one will ever know what you have done."

"I've seen all the statues I want to, thank you!" Emily laughed.

"Ain't no demon gods in London," Jack added proudly.

He scowled at Ben. "Except when they're brought in from foreign parts."

Ben laughed and aimed a lighthearted kick at Jack.

"And what waits for you in London, Señor Sherwood?" Roberto asked.

"What waits for me?" Edwin repeated thoughtfully. "Well, I'll be trying to rebuild my career as an archaeologist—since no one will believe me if I tell them what *really* happened—and enjoying life as a family man."

"Of course," Roberto said. "You have a young woman and a young man to look after now."

"Two young men," Edwin corrected him. "That is, if . . . well, if you still want to stay with us, Jack?"

Jack swallowed awkwardly and looked at the ground. He hadn't thought about it until now. The few months he had lived with Ben and Emily in Bedford Square had been great. Except for a few simple rules laid down by Mrs. Mills, they had been pretty much in charge of their own lives. But if Edwin was going to replace Ben and Emily's father, Jack thought, things might be different. He didn't want to be treated like a child. And he didn't want to get in the way.

"Don't need to be looked after all the time," he muttered dubiously.

"No," Edwin agreed, "but we all do *some* of the time, and the four of us have done a pretty good job of looking after one another so far. What do you say we keep up the good work?"

Jack looked up at Edwin, Ben, and Emily. They were all smiling at him, and a slow grin spread over his own face. He nodded shyly and Emily hugged him.

And then the skiff took them back to the Brotherhood's ship, which promptly hauled anchor and set sail. The friends waved at Roberto until he was just a dot on the horizon. Soon after that, Mexico, too, had vanished from sight.